ecret

Gabriel was weak. And there was a feeling inside him—a *hunger*. A burned-out feeling, like cracked earth thirsty for the summer rain.

He'd never felt like this before. And part of him said that there was something dangerous about feeling this way. Something *wrong*.

Ignore it, Gabriel thought—and then he saw the woman on the street. She was skin and bones, with hollow eyes and unhealthy hair. A tattoo of a unicorn covered the calf of one leg.

Now there was irony. A unicorn, the symbol of innocence.

Better this scrawny ratbag than the innocent witch back in the lot, he thought, and flashed his most brilliant, disturbing smile at nothing. Better her than Kaitlyn.

The burned, parched feeling was overwhelming him. He was a scorching void, an empty black hole. A starving wolf.

He put his hand on the woman's shoulder. . . .

Books by L.J. Smith

THE FORBIDDEN GAME, VOLUME I: THE HUNTER
THE FORBIDDEN GAME, VOLUME II: THE CHASE
THE FORBIDDEN GAME, VOLUME III: THE KILL
DARK VISIONS, VOLUME I: THE STRANGE POWER
DARK VISIONS, VOLUME II: THE POSSESSED
DARK VISIONS, VOLUME III: THE PASSION
NIGHT WORLD: SECRET VAMPIRE
NIGHT WORLD: DAUGHTERS OF DARKNESS
NIGHT WORLD: SPELLBINDER
NIGHT WORLD: DARK ANGEL
NIGHT WORLD: THE CHOSEN
NIGHT WORLD: SOULMATE
NIGHT WORLD: HUNTRESS
NIGHT WORLD: BLACK DAWN
NIGHT WORLD: WITCHLIGHT

Available from ARCHWAY Paperbacks

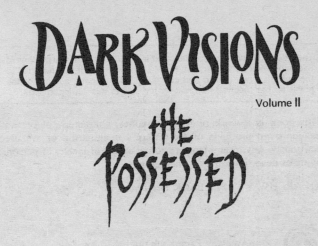

DARK VISIONS

Volume II

THE POSSESSED

L.J.SMITH

AN ARCHWAY PAPERBACK
Published by POCKET BOOKS
New York   London   Toronto   Sydney   Tokyo   Singapore

This book is a work of fiction. Names, characters, places and incidents are products of the author's imagination or are used fictitiously. Any resemblance to actual events or locales or persons, living or dead, is entirely coincidental.

AN ARCHWAY PAPERBACK *Original*

An Archway Paperback published by
POCKET BOOKS, a division of Simon & Schuster Inc.
1230 Avenue of the Americas, New York, NY 10020

ISBN: 0-671-87455-1

First Archway Paperback printing February 1995

10 9 8 7 6 5 4 3 2

AN ARCHWAY PAPERBACK and colophon are registered trademarks of Simon & Schuster Inc.

Cover art by Danilo Ducak

Printed in the U.S.A.

IL 7+

*For Rosemary Schmitt,
with thanks for all her good wishes
and support*

1

Hurry!" Kaitlyn gasped as she reached the top of the staircase. And she added with her mind, in case it might make more of an impression that way: *Hurry*.

From four different directions she felt acknowledgment, and an urgency just as strong as her own. Felt it with a sense that wasn't one of the ordinary five, but that was like seeing music or tasting color.

Telepathy was strange.

But sometimes comforting. Right now Kait was grateful for Rob's presence in her mind. It burned with a strong golden glow that warmed and steadied her. She could sense him in the next room, working fast but without panic, flipping through drawers and stuffing jeans and socks into a canvas bag.

They were leaving the Institute.

Not exactly the way they'd intended to, when they'd come to be part of a year-long psychic research project. Kaitlyn had expected to leave the Zetes

Institute next spring with a band playing, a college scholarship under her arm, and her father looking on proudly. Instead, she was scrambling in the middle of the night to get her belongings together and get out before Mr. Zetes caught up with them.

Mr. Zetes, the head of the Institute, the one who wanted to turn them into psychic weapons and sell them to the highest bidder.

Only maybe now he just wanted them dead. Because they'd found out what he was up to and fought back and beaten him. Impossible as that might sound, with all Mr. Z's power, they'd *won*. They'd left him knocked out cold in the secret rooms of his San Francisco mansion.

When he woke up he was going to be mad enough to kill.

"What are you taking?" Anna asked, and her usually calm voice had a hurried sound.

"I don't know. Clothes—warm clothes, I guess. We don't know where we'll be sleeping at night." Kait repeated the last thought mentally, so Rob and Lewis and Gabriel could hear. *Warm clothes, everybody!*

A mental voice answered her, sharp as a knife and cool as midnight. *And money,* it said. *Take all the money you can get your hands on.*

"Always practical, Gabriel," Kaitlyn murmured and stuffed her purse into a duffel bag, recklessly piling jeans and sweaters and underwear on top of it. She took her lucky hundred dollar bill out of a jewelry box on the dresser and jammed it in her pocket.

"What else?" she said aloud. She found herself grabbing crazy things: a velvet cap with gold embroidery, a necklace that had been her mother's, the paperback mystery she'd been reading. Finally she jammed in her smallest sketchbook and the plastic box that held her oil pastels and colored pencils. She *couldn't* leave without her art kit—she'd rather go naked.

And her drawings weren't just recreation; they were far more important than that. They were how she told the future.

Hurry, quick, she thought.

Anna was hesitating, looking at a carved wooden mask on the wall. It was Raven, the totem of Anna's family, and it was much too big to take with them.

"Anna . . ."

"I know." Anna touched the blunt beak of the mask once with graceful fingers, then turned from it. She smiled at Kaitlyn, her dark eyes serene over high cheekbones. "Let's go."

"Wait—soap." Kait dashed into the bathroom and snagged a bar of Ivory, catching a glimpse of herself in the mirror. Nothing like as serene as Anna—her long red hair was in elflocks, her cheeks were flushed, and the strange blue rings in her eyes were burning smokily. She looked like a feverish witch.

"Okay," Rob said as they all met in the hall. "Everybody ready?"

Kaitlyn looked at them, at the four people who'd become closer to her than she would have imagined any people could be.

Rob Kessler, all warmth and color, gold-blond hair and golden eyes. Gabriel Wolfe, arrogant and handsome, like a drawing done in black and white. Anna Eva Whiteraven, her expression gentle even under pressure. Lewis Chao with his almond-shaped eyes glittering with anxiety, slapping a baseball cap onto smooth black hair.

Thanks to Gabriel's power going out of control, they were linked by a telepathic web. None of them would ever be alone again—unless they could find a way to break the link.

"I want to get something from downstairs," Gabriel was saying.

"Me, too," Rob said, "and I need Lewis to help. All right, let's get moving. You all right, Kait?"

"Just breathless," Kaitlyn said. Her heart was pounding, and there was a shakiness in every limb that made her not want to stand still.

Rob reached to take her duffel bag with the ruthless courtesy of his North Carolina lineage. For just an instant their hands touched; his strong fingers wrapped around hers.

It'll be all right, he told her in a swift private communication meant for no one else.

The feeling that flooded Kaitlyn was almost painful. For God's sake, not *now,* she thought and ignored the sparks that swarmed where he'd touched her skin.

"Be careful, you—healer," she said and started down the stairs.

Lewis kept glancing over his shoulder. "My computer," he mourned softly. "My stereo, my TV set . . ."

"Why don't you go back and get them?" Gabriel asked nastily. "What could be more inconspicuous?"

"Keep *moving,"* Rob ordered. At the bottom of the stairs he said, "Lewis, come with me."

Kait followed them. "What are you doing?"

4

"Getting the files," Rob said grimly. "Okay, Lewis, open that panel."

Of course, Kaitlyn thought. Mr. Zetes's files, the ones he kept in the hidden room here under the stairway. They were full of all kinds of information, most of it cryptic, some of it undoubtedly incriminating.

"But what can we *do* with them? Who can we show them to?"

"I don't know," Rob said. "But I want them anyway. They *prove* what he's been up to."

Lewis was running sensitive fingertips over the dark paneling on the wall. Kaitlyn could feel what he was doing, trying to locate the spring release with his mind. "It's not easy to perform on demand like this," he muttered, but then there was a click and the panel slid back.

"Mind over matter," Rob said, grinning.

Hurry, Kaitlyn told him sharply.

She didn't wait to see him start down into the dimly lit hallway behind the door. She took her duffel bag into the front laboratory where Anna was opening a wire cage.

"Go on," she was saying. "Go on, Georgie Mouse, go on, Sally Mouse . . ." She knelt to hold the cage by the open side door.

"You're letting them out?"

"I'm *sending* them away, telling them to find a field. I don't know what Mr. Z will do to them," Anna said. "I don't even trust Joyce anymore." Joyce Piper was the parapsychologist who actually ran the Institute for Mr. Zetes, the one who'd recruited Kaitlyn. Even

5

now, Kaitlyn couldn't think about her without feeling a twinge of betrayal.

"Okay, but *hurry*. We don't have time to waste," she said and moved restlessly back into the hallway. Lewis was tugging at his baseball cap nervously.

Gabriel, in the small bedroom beyond, was going through Joyce's purse.

Gabriel! Kait said. She could feel her shock reverberating in the telepathic web, and she tried to muffle it.

He merely slanted her an ironic glance. "We need money."

"But you can't—"

"Why not?" he said. His gray eyes were so dark they looked almost black.

"Because it isn't . . . it's not . . ." Kaitlyn could feel herself sagging. "It's wrong," she said finally.

Gabriel didn't admit to concepts like "wrong."

"Joyce is our enemy," he said shortly. "If it wasn't for her, we wouldn't be running away in the middle of the night in the first place. It's necessary—and you know it, don't you, Kait?"

It was dangerous to look into Gabriel's eyes for more than an instant. Kaitlyn turned away without answering, then turned back to hiss, "All right, but don't take any credit cards. They can trace those. And don't let Rob know, or he'll go ballistic. And *hurry.*"

That one word had begun to pound relentlessly in her brain: hurry, hurry, hurry. Faster than a heartbeat. She had a feeling—no, a certainty—that every second they stayed here was too long.

A premonition? But she didn't have that kind of

premonition. It was only by drawing that she could get an image of the future.

Hurry. Hurry. Hurry.

Trust yourself, she thought suddenly. Go with your feelings.

"Gabriel," she said abruptly, "we've got to leave now." She added in an urgent mental shout, *Lewis, Rob, Anna—we have to leave! Right now, this second! Something's going to happen—I don't know what, but we've got to get out of here—*

"Take it easy." She felt Gabriel's hand on her arm and only then realized how agitated she was. As soon as she'd spoken her feelings out loud, she'd realized how strong they were, how urgent.

"I'm all right, but Gabriel, we've got to go. . . ."

He looked into her eyes briefly and nodded. "If you feel like that—come on."

In the hallway Rob was hurrying out of the open panel with an armful of file folders. Anna was emerging from the lab.

"What's wrong? Is someone coming?" Rob asked.

"I don't know, I just know we have to hurry—"

"We'll take Joyce's car," Gabriel said.

Rob hesitated, then nodded. "Come on, out the back door." He hustled Lewis and Anna ahead of him. Kaitlyn followed right on his heels, feeling she couldn't move fast enough.

"We'll just use the car to get out of the area," Rob was saying, when a wave of adrenaline broke over Kaitlyn. It left a metallic taste of fear in her mouth.

Behind her the front door burst open.

2

Kaitlyn looked back.

Mr. Zetes.

Light from the porch shone behind him so he appeared as a dark silhouette, but somehow Kait could still see his face. When she'd first come to the Institute a week ago, she'd thought that Mr. Z was a handsome, aristocratic old gentleman—like Little Lord Fauntleroy's grandfather. Now she knew the truth, and the leonine head with its shock of white hair appeared completely evil to her. Those piercing dark eyes seemed to burn like—

Like a demon's, Kaitlyn thought. Except he's not a demon, just an insane genius, and we've got to get *out* of here. . . .

They were all paralyzed. Even Gabriel, who was in front of Kaitlyn now that she had turned around, closer to Mr. Zetes. Something about the man stopped them all dead, drained the will out of them.

They were held by pure fear.

Don't look at him, Rob's voice said in Kaitlyn's mind, but it was faint and distant. The terror reverberating in the web was much stronger.

"Come here," Mr. Zetes said. His voice was strong and rich and utterly commanding. He stepped forward and Kaitlyn could see him more clearly in the living room lights. There was blood in his thick white hair and on his starched shirt collar. Gabriel's mental attack had done that, knocked him out, made him bleed. But Gabriel was exhausted now. . . .

As if he were part of the web and could hear her thoughts, Mr. Zetes said, "You're all tired. I don't think you can use your powers any further tonight. Why don't we sit down and talk together?"

Kait had been too frightened to speak, but this struck fire in her. "We don't have anything to talk about," she said caustically.

"Your futures," Mr. Zetes said. "Your lives. I realize that I was too harsh earlier tonight. It was a shock to find you'd gotten yourselves into a permanent telepathic link. But I still think we can work together. We'll find another way to break the link—"

"You mean besides killing one of us?" Kaitlyn snarled.

Don't stick around and argue with him, Gabriel said, his cold mental voice cutting through the thrumming fear in the web. *You four go—start heading for the back door. I'll keep him here.*

"No," Kaitlyn said aloud, before she could help it. Even in the middle of this danger, she felt a wash of emotion. Gabriel, who'd always claimed he didn't care about anybody, was risking himself to protect them. . . .

And he was moving now, putting himself directly between her and Mr. Zetes. Once she could no longer see Mr. Zetes's face, she felt her paralysis break.

But we can't leave you, she told Gabriel. *You nearly died once tonight already—*

Gabriel didn't glance back. His posture was wolf-like, his attention fixed on Mr. Zetes. *Kessler, get them out. I'll handle the old man.*

But Rob's mental voice was sharp. *No! None of us can stay. Don't you see, he wants to keep us here—and we haven't seen Joyce yet.*

The instant he said it, Kaitlyn knew he was right. It was a trap.

"Come on!" she shouted, both mentally and aloud —but even as she was shouting it, a shape appeared in the kitchen doorway beside her. Hands grabbed for her.

"Let me go!"

Kait found herself kicking and screaming. Other shouts hurt her ears. All she could see was the venemous, twisted face in front of her.

Joyce Piper's sleek blond hair was plastered flat to her head with sweat and blood. Dried rivulets ran down her cheeks. Her aquamarine eyes were full of heated poison, and her lips were drawn back.

Oh, God, she wants to kill me; she really wants to kill me. I trusted her and she's crazy, she's as crazy as Mr. Zetes is—

Hands were pulling her away from Joyce, shoving her toward the back of the house. Rob's voice rose over the background shouting.

"Run, Kaitlyn! Go! Everybody run!"

Looking back, Kaitlyn had a brief glimpse of Rob

and Gabriel grappling with Joyce, of Mr. Zetes coming toward them, his face suffused with fury. Then she was running, with Lewis and Anna jostling around her. She didn't realize she still had her duffel bag until she got to the back door and had to put it down to undo the locks.

She yanked the door open—and there was Mr. Zetes's chauffeur. Looking immovable as a mountain, blocking the way.

Get him!

Kaitlyn wasn't sure who shouted it, but she and Anna and Lewis were all moving at once. It was as if they suddenly had only one mind, divided into three bodies. Lewis put his head down and ran at the man's stomach; Kait swung her duffel bag at his face; Anna slammed a foot into his shin. He toppled over and they ran on, stampeding toward the green convertible in the driveway.

It was Joyce's car, the car they'd taken from Mr. Zetes's mansion to get back to the Institute. The keys were still inside.

"Get in the back," Kaitlyn told Lewis and Anna, throwing her duffel bag into the backseat. *Rob! Gabriel! Get out here! Come on; we're ready for you!*

She twisted the key in the ignition, yanked at the gearshift, and turned the wheel hard. She wasn't a very good driver—she hadn't had much practice back in Ohio—but now she sent gravel flying as she swung the convertible in a tight arc on the driveway.

"Headlights—" Lewis gasped. Kait reached down blindly and wrenched a dial. The blaze of light illuminated the chauffeur, who was on his feet again in front of them.

Kaitlyn headed right toward him.

She could hear yelling, but everything seemed to be happening in slow motion. The chauffeur's mouth was open. For endless seconds the car kept getting closer and closer to him, and then suddenly he was diving sideways. He got out of the way just as Rob and Gabriel burst through the back door.

Get in! Kait hit the brake, jolting the car. Rob and Gabriel scrambled in, climbing over Lewis and Anna. Kaitlyn didn't wait for them to untangle themselves; she put her foot on the accelerator and pressed—hard.

Go, she was thinking—or maybe it was somebody else thinking it, she couldn't tell. *Go, go, go, go.*

Tires squealed as she reached the street, turned, and sped away from the purple house that was the Zetes Institute for Psychic Research.

It was a great relief to be moving this fast. She overshot stop signs, shrieked around corners. She didn't know where she was going, just that she had to get as far away as possible.

"Kait." It was Rob's voice. Rob was in the front seat beside her, an armful of folders clutched to his chest. He put a hand on her arm. *Kait.*

Kaitlyn was breathing hard and shivering—a fine all-over tremor. She'd reached El Camino Real, the main street in San Carlos. She ran a red light.

Kait, ease up. We got away. It's all right. His fingers tightened on her arm, and he repeated, "It's all right."

Kaitlyn felt her breath come out more slowly. She was able to ease her grip on the steering wheel. "Are you guys okay?"

"Yeah," Rob said. "Gabriel knocked them out

again. They're both lying unconscious in the lab." He turned to look into the backseat. "Nice going."

"Oh, glad you thought so," Gabriel said in a voice as cold as Rob's had been warm. But through the web, Kaitlyn could feel Gabriel's desperate tiredness.

She sensed a rush of concern from Rob and knew he felt it, too. "Look," he said, "you're wiped out. Do you want me to—"

No, Gabriel said flatly.

Kaitlyn's heart sank. Just an hour or so ago Gabriel had been willing to accept Rob's help—all their help. Back at the mansion he'd let Rob use his healing power, let him channel energy from the rest of them to save Gabriel's life. Gabriel had come to trust all of them, when he'd never trusted anyone before. They'd actually gotten through to him, broken down the walls. And now . . .

Gabriel was reverting again. Shutting them out, pretending he wasn't part of them. And there was nothing they could do about it.

Kaitlyn gave it a try anyway. Sometimes Gabriel seemed to . . . respect her more than the others, or at least he listened to her opinions more. "You've got to keep your strength up," she began lightly, trying to catch his eye in the rearview mirror.

He cut her off with a terse, *Leave me alone.*

Kait got an image of walls, high walls with nasty spikes sticking out of them. Gabriel trying to cover his vulnerability. She knew what he wouldn't verbalize, that he didn't want to be indebted to Rob ever again.

Anna's quiet voice broke into her thoughts. "Where are we going?"

"I don't know." It was a good question and Kait's

heart started pounding again. "You guys, where *can* we go?"

She could sense consternation all around her. None of them except Lewis was familiar with the San Francisco area.

"Well—jeeez," Lewis said. "Okay, we don't want to go into the city, right? My parents live up in Pacific Heights, but—"

"But that's the first place Mr. Z will look," Rob said. "No, we agreed before, we can't go to our parents. We'll only get them in trouble, too."

"The truth is," Gabriel began, "we don't know *where* we're going—"

"It doesn't matter," Kaitlyn interrupted him. "It doesn't matter where we're going eventually. What we need to figure out is what to do *now*. It's two A.M. and it's dark and it's cold and Mr. Zetes is going to be after us . . ."

"You're right about that," Gabriel said. "And he'll have the police after us, too, when he wakes up from being knocked out. We're in a stolen car."

"Then we'd better get away from San Carlos fast," Lewis said, alarm sharpening his voice. "There's Highway 101, Kait. Get on it going north."

Kaitlyn clenched her teeth and got on the freeway, which was a big one, five lanes in each direction. She knew the others must be aware of how nervous she was, but no one mentioned it.

"Now, let's see . . . we don't want to go to San Francisco. . . . Okay, take the San Mateo bridge there, and when you get across, go on 880 north. That's the East Bay; you know, Hayward and Oakland."

The bridge started out wide but narrowed to a

ribbon of concrete that seemed to barely clear dark water. In a few minutes they were cruising up another freeway.

"Good job," Rob said softly, and Kaitlyn felt a flash of warmth. "Now, don't speed too much; we don't want to draw attention to ourselves."

Kaitlyn nodded and kept the red hand of the speedometer quivering just below sixty miles per hour. They hadn't been driving two minutes before Lewis said, "Uh-oh."

"What 'uh-oh?'" Kaitlyn asked tightly.

"There's a car behind us with antlers," Anna said. *"Antlers?"*

"Police light bar," Lewis said. His voice was thin.

Rob stayed calm. "Don't panic. They won't pull you over for going three miles over the speed limit, and Mr. Z probably isn't even awake yet. . . ."

Lights sprang to life on the roof of the car behind Kaitlyn. Blue and yellow flashing lights.

Kaitlyn's stomach plunged as if she'd stepped into an elevator. Her heart had begun a sick pounding.

"Can we panic now?" Lewis gasped. "I thought you said Mr. Z wouldn't be awake yet."

"We forgot," Anna said. "He had plenty of time to call the police and report the car stolen back at the mansion. When he *first* woke up."

Kait had a wild impulse to run. She'd run from the police a time or two back in Ohio, mainly when they wanted her to make some prediction about a case they were working on. But that had been on foot, out in the farmland that surrounded Thoroughfare—and she hadn't been a criminal then.

Now she was in a stolen car, and she'd just helped assault three grown-ups.

And you've got me *in the car, and I'm violating my parole,* Gabriel's voice said in her mind. *Remember? I'm not supposed to leave the Institute except to go to school.*

"Oh, God," Kaitlyn said aloud. She gripped the wheel with palms that were slick with sweat. The need to run, to jam on the accelerator and get *out* of here, was swelling in her like a balloon.

"No," Rob said urgently. "We won't be able to get away from them, and the last thing we want is a high-speed chase."

"Then what do we do, Rob?" Anna asked.

"Pull over." Rob looked at Kait. "Pull over and we'll talk to them. I'll show them *this.*" He hefted the files. "And if they take us to the police station, I'll show it to everyone there."

Kaitlyn felt a surge of incredulity from Gabriel. "Are you joking? How naive are you, Kessler? Do you think anybody is going to believe five kids—especially any cop—" He broke off. When he spoke again, it was in a different voice, taut and yet somehow expressionless. "Fine. Pull over, Kait."

Walls. Kait could feel Gabriel's walls go up, but she had more critical things to think about. She took the next exit off the freeway and the flashing blue and yellow lights followed her.

She went quite a way down the street before she could make herself slow and stop. The police car glided up behind her like a shark and stopped, too.

Kaitlyn was breathing hard. "Okay, you guys . . ."

"I'll do the talking," Rob said, and Kait was grateful. She watched in the rearview mirror as a figure got out of the cruiser. There was only one officer, a policeman.

With numb fingers, Kaitlyn rolled down the window. The policeman bent down a bit. He had a neat dark mustache and a very solid-looking chin.

"Driver's license," he said, and Rob, leaning over Kait, said, "Excuse me." And then Kait felt it.

A pulling-back, like the ocean gathering for a tsunami. It came from the backseat. Before she could move or say anything, Gabriel struck.

Dark power shot out of him toward the policeman, a wave of crashing, destructive mental energy. The policeman made a sound like a hurt animal and dropped his notebook, clapping his hands to his head.

"No!" Rob shouted. "Gabriel, stop!"

Kaitlyn could only feel the echoes of the attack through the web, but it was blinding her, making her sick. Dimly she saw the policeman fall to his knees. Anna was gasping. Lewis was whimpering.

Gabriel, stop! Rob roared in a voice to cut through all the confusion. *You'll kill him. Stop!*

I have to help him, Kaitlyn thought. We can't become murderers . . . I have to help. . . .

It took a tremendous effort of will to turn around, to focus on Gabriel's mind. She wanted to shield herself from the terrible power still pouring out of Gabriel. Instead, she opened herself to it, trying to break through to him.

Gabriel, you're not a killer, not anymore, she told him. *Please stop. Please stop.*

17

She had a sense of wavering, and then the black torrent eased. It seemed to flow back into Gabriel, where it disappeared without a trace.

Trembling, Kaitlyn leaned her head against the seat back. There was absolute silence in the car.

Then Rob erupted. *"Why?* Why did you *do* that?"

"Because he would never have listened to us. Nobody's going to listen, Kessler. Nobody's on our side. We've got to *fight* if we want to live. But you don't know anything about that, do you?"

"I'll show *you* something about it—"

"Stop it!" Kaitlyn shouted, grabbing Rob, who was lunging at Gabriel. "Shut up, both of you. We don't have time to fight—we've got to get out of here, now." She fumbled with the door handle and flung the door open, dragging her duffel bag behind her.

The policeman was lying still now, but to Kaitlyn's relief he was breathing.

Who knows if his mind's okay, though, she thought. Gabriel's power could drive people into screaming insanity.

The others were scrambling out of the car. Lewis was ghastly pale in the police car's headlights, and Anna's dark eyes were huge—owl eyes. When Rob knelt by the policeman, Kaitlyn could feel the tension in his body.

Rob passed a hand over the policeman's chest. "I think he'll be all right—"

"Then let's *go,"* Kaitlyn said, casting a desperate look around and pulling at him. "Before somebody sees us, before they send more police . . ."

"Take his badge first," Gabriel suggested nastily, and that got Rob on his feet. And then something seemed to break in all of them simultaneously, and they were running away from the deserted police car.

At first Kaitlyn didn't care where she was running. Gabriel was in the lead, and she blindly followed his twists and turns onto side streets. Eventually, though, when a stabbing pain in her side slowed her down to a walk, she began to notice her surroundings.

Oh, God, where *are* we?

"It's not Mister Rogers' neighborhood," Lewis muttered and jammed his baseball cap on backward.

It was the most eerie and menacing street Kait had ever seen. The gas station they were passing was derelict: no glass in the windows, no gas pumps. So was the station across the road. The Dairy Belle snack shop was enclosed by a very solid-looking chain-link fence—a fence that had barbed wire on the top.

Beyond the Dairy Belle was a liquor store with a flickering yellow sign and iron bars in front of the glass windows. It was open and several men stood in the doorway. Kaitlyn saw one of them look across the street—directly at her.

She couldn't see his face, but she saw teeth flash in a grin. The man elbowed one of his companions, then took a step toward the street.

3

Kaitlyn froze, her legs suddenly refusing to move. Rob moved up beside her, put an arm around her, urging her on. "Anna, come here," he said quietly, and Anna obeyed without a word. Lewis crowded up close.

The man across the street had stopped, but he was still watching them.

"Just go on walking," Rob said. "Don't look back." There was calm conviction in his voice, and the arm around Kait's shoulders was hard with muscle.

Gabriel turned around to sneer. "What's the matter, Kessler? Scared?"

I'm scared, Kaitlyn told him, before Rob could respond. She could feel Rob's anger—he and Gabriel were spoiling for a fight. *I'm scared of this place, and I don't want to stay here all night.*

"Well, why didn't you say so?" Gabriel nodded down the street. "Let's go there, where the factories

20

are. We'll find some place to hole up where the cops won't find us."

They crossed railroad tracks, passed huge warehouses and yards full of trucks. Kaitlyn kept glancing behind her nervously, but the only sign of life here was the white smoke billowing out of the Granny Goose factory's smokestacks.

"Here," Gabriel said abruptly. It was a vacant lot, fenced and barb-wired like everything else around here. A sign inside read:

SALE LEASE 4+ ACRES
APPROX. 180,000 SQ. FEET
PACIFIC AMERICAN GROUP

Gabriel was standing by a gate in the fence, and Kaitlyn saw that the barbed wire on top of the gate was squashed flat. "Give me a sweater or something," he said. Kaitlyn took off her ski jacket, and Gabriel spread it over the flattened barbed wire.

"Now climb."

In another minute they were inside the lot, and Kait had her jacket back—now dotted with perforations. She didn't care; all she wanted to do was huddle down like a duckling in some place where nothing could get her.

The lot was a good place. A huge rampart of dirt clods screened the middle of it off from the street. Kaitlyn stumbled over to a corner where two walls of dirt met and collapsed against it. The adrenaline that had fueled her for the last eight or nine hours had run out, leaving every muscle like jelly.

"I'm so tired," she whispered.

"We all are," Rob said, sitting beside her. "Come on, Gabriel, get down before somebody sees you. You're half dead."

Right, Kaitlyn thought. Gabriel had been exhausted before knocking out the policeman, and now he was almost shaking with fatigue.

He stayed on his feet for a moment, just to prove that he wasn't listening to Rob, then sat down. He sat across from the rest of them, keeping his distance.

Lewis and Anna, though, scooted in close to Kaitlyn. She shut her eyes and leaned back, glad of their closeness, and of Rob. Rob's warm, solid body seemed to radiate protectiveness. He won't let anyone hurt me, she thought foggily.

No, I won't, Rob's voice in her mind said, and she felt immersed in gold. An amber glow that warmed her and even fed her, somehow, pouring radiance into her. Like cuddling up with a sun, she thought.

I'm so tired. . . .

She opened her eyes. "Are we going to sleep here?"

"I think we'd better," Rob said, his voice dragging. "But maybe one of us should stay up—you know, to keep watch in case somebody comes."

"I'll watch," Gabriel said briefly.

"No." Kaitlyn was appalled. "You need sleep more than any of us. . . ."

Not sleep. The thought was so fleeting, so faint, that Kaitlyn wasn't sure if she'd really heard it or not. Gabriel was the best at screening his thoughts from the rest of them. Right now Kaitlyn could sense nothing from him in the web, except that he was drained. And that he was adamant.

"Go ahead, Gabriel, suit yourself," Rob was saying grimly.

Kaitlyn was too tired to argue with either of them. She'd never imagined that she could sleep outdoors like this, sitting on the bare ground with nothing over her head. But it had been the longest night of her life—and the *worst*—and the dirt wall behind her felt amazingly comfortable. Anna was pressed up against her on one side and Rob on the other. The March night was mild and her ski jacket kept her warm. She felt—almost safe.

Kaitlyn's eyes closed.

Now I know what it's like to be homeless, she thought. Uprooted, out in the world, adrift. Heck, I *am* homeless.

"What city are we in?" she mumbled, feeling somehow that this was important.

"Oakland, I guess," Lewis muttered back. "Hear the planes? We must be near the airport."

Kaitlyn could hear a plane, and crickets, and distant traffic—but they all seemed to be fading into a featureless hum. In a few moments she stopped thinking and was dreaming instead.

Gabriel waited until all four of them were asleep—fast asleep—and then he stood up.

He supposed he was putting them in danger by leaving. Well, he couldn't help it—and if Kessler couldn't protect his girl, that was his own lookout.

It had become painfully obvious that Kaitlyn was Kessler's girl now. Fine. Gabriel didn't want her anyway. He should be grateful to Rob the Golden Boy for saving him—because a girl like that could trap you, could get under your skin and change you. And this particular girl, with hair like autumn fire and skin like cream and the eyes of a witch, had already shown that she wanted to change *him*.

Almost succeeded, too, Gabriel thought as he picked his way through the scraggly brush poking its way between dirt clods. She'd gotten him in a state to accept help from Kessler, of all people.

Never again.

Gabriel reached the fence and boosted himself over it, clearing the barbed wire. When he came down, his knees almost buckled.

He was weak. Weak in a way he'd never been before. And there was a feeling inside him—a *hunger*. A burned-out feeling, as if a fire had passed over him, leaving him blackened and parched. Like cracked earth thirsty for summer rain.

He'd never felt like this before. And part of him, a small part that sat back from the rest of his mind and sometimes whispered judgment, said that there was something dangerous about feeling this way. Something *wrong*.

Ignore it, Gabriel thought. He made his legs move down the uneven sidewalk, tightening muscles so they wouldn't shake. He wasn't afraid of this kind of neighborhood—it was his native environment—but he knew better than to show weakness here. The weak got picked off in a place like this.

He was looking for someone else weak.

The whispering part of his mind twinged at that.

Ignore it, Gabriel thought again.

The liquor store was up ahead. Beside it was a long brick wall decorated with the remains of tattered posters and notices. Men stood against the wall, or sat on crates in front of it.

Men—and one woman. Not a beauty. She was skin and bones, with hollow eyes and unhealthy hair. A tattoo of a unicorn covered the calf of one leg.

Now there was irony. A unicorn, the symbol of innocence, virginity.

Better this scrawny ratbag than the innocent witch back in the lot, he thought, and flashed his most brilliant, disturbing smile at nothing.

That thought demolished the last of his hesitation. It had to be someone. He'd rather it be this bit of human garbage than Kaitlyn.

The burned, parched feeling was overwhelming him. He was a scorching void, an empty black hole. A starving wolf.

The woman turned toward him. She looked startled for a moment, then smiled in appreciation, her eyes on his face.

Think I'm handsome? Good, that makes it easy, Gabriel thought, smiling back.

He put his hand on her shoulder.

The ocean hissed and spat among the rocks. The sky was an uneasy color, more metallic violet or grayed lavender than real gray, Kaitlyn thought. She was standing on a narrow rocky peninsula. On either side of her was the ocean. Ahead the peninsula stretched out like a bony finger into the water.

A strange place. A strange and lonely place . . .

"Oh, no. Here *again?*" Lewis said from just behind her.

Kait turned to see him—and Rob and Anna, as

well. She smiled. The first time she'd found them in her dream she'd been confused and almost angry. Now she didn't mind; she was glad of the company.

"At least it's not so cold this time," Anna said. She looked as if she fit into this wild place where nature seemed to rule without human interference. The wind blew her long dark hair behind her.

"No, and we should be *glad* to be here," Rob said, his voice full of suppressed excitement. He was scanning the horizon alertly. "This is where we're *going,* remember—if we can find it."

"No," Kait said. *"That's* where we're going." She pointed across the water to a distant shore where a cliff rose, black with thick-growing trees. Among the trees, shining in the eerie light, was a single white house.

It was the white house Kaitlyn had seen in a vision at the Institute. The one in the photograph shown to her by a lynx-eyed man with caramel-colored skin. She knew nothing about the man except that he was an enemy of Mr. Zetes, and nothing about the house except that it was connected to the man.

"But it's our only chance," she said aloud. The others were looking at her, and she went on, "We don't know who they are, but they're the only people who even have a chance to help us against Mr. Z. We don't have any choice but to try and find them."

"And maybe they can help us with"—Lewis changed to telepathic speech in midsentence—*this thing. Maybe they'll know how to break the link.*

Anna spoke quietly. "You know what the research says. One of us has to die."

"Maybe they can find some way around that."

Kaitlyn said nothing, but she knew they all felt the same way. The web that tied them together had brought them very close, and there were some wonderful things about it. But all the same, in the back of her mind there was always the pounding insistence that it *had* to be broken. They couldn't live the rest of their lives like this, welded together this way. They *couldn't*. . . .

"We'll find the answers when we get there," Rob said. "Meanwhile, we'd better look around. Examine everything about this place. There must be some clue as to where it *is*."

"Let's walk up there," Kait suggested, nodding toward the end of the peninsula. "I'd like to get as close to that house as possible."

They kept a close watch as they walked. "Same old ocean," Lewis said. "And back there"—he gestured behind them—"same old beach with trees. If I had my camera we could get a photo to compare to other things. Like, you know, pictures in books or travel brochures."

"There's just not enough to distinguish it from other beaches," Kaitlyn said. "Except—look, does it seem to you that there are more waves on the right side?"

"It does," Rob said. "That's weird. I wonder what would cause it?"

"And then there are these," said Anna. She dropped to one knee beside a pile of rocks, some long and thin, some nearly square. They were stacked like a child's blocks, but much more whimsically, forming an irregular tower that had appendages sticking out at intervals—like airplane wings.

The piles were all over the peninsula, resting on the huge boulders that lined either side. They ranged from small to gargantuan. Some, to Kaitlyn's eye, looked like crude depictions of people or animals.

"I have the feeling I should *know* this," Anna said, her hands framing the stack, not quite touching it. "It should have some meaning to me." Her face was troubled, her full lips pinched, her eyes clouded.

"Never mind," Rob said. "Keep walking and maybe it'll come to you. Is it a place you've seen before?"

Anna shook her head slowly. "I don't *think* I've seen it. And yet it's *familiar*—and it's north, I'm sure of that. North of California."

"So we look at all the beaches north of California?" Lewis muttered, with unaccustomed bleakness. He kicked at a rock pile.

"Don't!" Anna said quickly—with unaccustomed sharpness. Lewis ducked his head.

At the end of the peninsula Kait tilted her face to the wind. It felt good and it was exhilarating to have the ocean crashing around her on three sides, but they still weren't much closer to the white house.

"Who's giving us these dreams, anyway?" Lewis asked from a little way behind her. "I mean, do you think it's *them*, in that house? Do you think they're in there now?"

"Let's ask," Rob said, and without warning he cupped his hands around his mouth and shouted across the water. "Hey, you! You out there! Who are you?"

Kaitlyn's heart jolted at the first bellow. But the shout had a *good* sound, a sound to combat the ghostly violet sky and the vast stretch of moving water. This was a big place, and big sounds fit here.

She cupped her own hands around her mouth. "Whooo are yooooou?" she shouted, sending her voice across the ocean as if she really expected someone in the white house to hear.

"That's it," Anna said, and she threw her head back and gave a long-drawn-out cry that sent gooseflesh up Kait's spine. "Whooo are yooooou? Where are weeee?"

Lewis joined in. "Thiiiis suuucks! Talk to us! Can't you be a little clearer?"

Kaitlyn choked on laughter, but kept calling. The racket caused a pair of gulls to soar upward, alarmed.

And then, amidst their own clamor, came an answer.

It was louder than their shouting voices, but it was a breathless whisper nevertheless. As if, Kaitlyn thought suddenly, a thousand people were whispering at once, almost in chorus but not quite. A thousand people crowded around you in a small, echoing room.

It shut them all up immediately. Kait stared wide-eyed at Rob, who had grasped her shoulder in an automatic impulse to protect her.

"Griffin's Pit! Griffin's Pit! Griffin's Pit!" the urgent whispers said.

Kaitlyn's lips formed the word "What?" but no sound came out. The cacophony of sound was beating at her from all sides. She could see Lewis grimace. Anna had her hands to her head.

"Griffin's Pit Griffin's Pit Griffin's Pit . . ."

Rob, it hurts. . . .

Then wake up, Kaitlyn! It's your dream; you have to wake up!

She couldn't. But she could see that the pounding noise was hurting Rob, too. His face was tense, his golden eyes dark.

"GriffinsPitGriffinsPitGriffinsPit—"

Kaitlyn gave a jerk and the peninsula disappeared.

She was staring into the night sky. A lopsided moon was dipping toward the horizon. A single airplane roared slowly among the stars, red lights winking.

Rob was stirring beside her, Anna and Lewis sitting up.

"Everybody all right?" Kaitlyn said anxiously.

Rob smiled. "You did it."

"I guess. And we got our answer—I guess." She rubbed at her forehead.

"Maybe that's why they didn't try to communicate in words before," Anna said. "Maybe they knew it would hurt us. And what they were saying wasn't too clear, anyway."

"Griffin's Pit," Kaitlyn said. "It sounds—ominous."

Lewis wrinkled his nose. "Griffin's—*what?* Oh, you mean Whippin' Bit."

"*I* heard something like 'Wyvern's Bit,'" Anna put in. "But that doesn't make much sense."

"Neither does Whiff and Spit," Rob said. "Unless it's some kind of combination perfume and tobacco factory. . . ."

"C'mon down to the Whiff and Spit; snuff it up and cough it out," Lewis chanted, giving it a catchy

30

rhythm. "But, look, if none of us heard the same thing, it means we're back where we started."

"Wrong," Rob said and twisted Lewis's cap down over his eyes. He grinned; Kaitlyn could tell he was in a good mood. "We know there's somebody out there, and they're trying to talk to us. Maybe they'll get better. Maybe we'll get lucky. Anyway, we have a direction to go—north. And we know what to look for—a beach like that. The search is on!"

His enthusiasm was infectious. His smile, the lights dancing in his golden eyes—all infectious, Kaitlyn thought.

Kaitlyn had a feeling—wild, inappropriate, but consuming—of hope. All her life she'd wanted to belong somewhere, wanted it with a deep-down, gut-wrenching ache. And she'd always had the strange conviction that she *did* belong somewhere. That there was a place where she fit in perfectly—if only she could find it.

Since Gabriel had locked them into the web, she'd found *people* to belong to. Whether she wanted it or not, she was bonded for life to her four mind-mates. And now—well, maybe the dream was calling them to a *place* to belong. The place she'd sensed in the back of her mind all along, the place where all her questions would be answered and she would understand who she really was and what she was supposed to do with her life.

She smiled at Rob. "The search is on." She scooted closer to him, knee to knee, and added in a private message, *And I love you.*

Strange coincidence, Rob's voice said in her mind. Amazing how he could make her feel. Safe in a vacant lot, warm in the middle of the night. Just being this close to him, being able to touch his thoughts and feel his presence, was comforting—and dizzying.

I like being close to you, too, he said. *The closer I get, the closer I want to get.*

Kaitlyn was floating, drowning in the gold of Rob's eyes. She began, *I wish we could be like this forever*—

She was cut off. Anna, who had been sitting with her chin on her knees, now suddenly raised her head. "Wait a minute—where's Gabriel?"

Kait had forgotten about him. Now she realized that the rampart of earth across from them was deserted.

"He must have gone to check on something," Lewis said hopefully.

"Or maybe he's gone for good," Rob said—and there was a sort of grim hope in his voice, too.

"Sorry. No deal." A shower of earth fell from the dirt wall, and Gabriel appeared, wearing a rather chilling smile.

And he looked—well. Refreshed. Not tired anymore.

Kaitlyn felt the shadow of alarm. She brushed it away before anyone else could notice it. Of *course* Gabriel was all right. There was nothing wrong with him looking so . . . rejuvenated. He'd had a chance to rest, that was all.

"It's getting light," Gabriel was saying. "I checked around; there's no activity out there: no cops, nothing. If we're going to get out, now's the time."

"Okay," Rob said. "But first, sit down a minute. We have to figure out what the plan is, what we're doing next. And we have to tell you what happened to us tonight."

"Something happened?" Gabriel looked around sharply. "I was—only gone for a few minutes."

"It wasn't anything real; it was a dream," Kaitlyn said, and she tried to quash her alarm again. That hesitation between "I was" and "only gone for a few minutes"—Gabriel was lying. She couldn't feel it in the web, but she knew.

Where had he been?

Rob was telling him about the dream. Gabriel listened to the whole story, looking amused and slightly contemptuous.

"If that's where you really think you're going, I don't care," he said when Rob finished. His handsome lip was curled. "All I care about is getting away from the California Youth Authority."

"Okay," said Rob. "Now, we ought to take stock—what have we got with us here? What're our assets?" He gave a rueful grin. "'Fraid I don't have anything but my wallet and these files."

For the first time Kait consciously realized that neither Rob nor Gabriel had their duffel bags with them. Lost in the fight with Mr. Zetes, she guessed.

"I've got my bag," she said. "And a hundred dollars in my pocket"—she checked to make sure—"and maybe fifteen in my purse."

"I've got *my* bag," Lewis said. "But I don't think any of my clothes are going to fit either of you guys." He eyed Rob and Gabriel doubtfully—they were both several inches taller than he was. "And about forty dollars."

"I've only got a few dollars in change," Anna said. "And my bag of clothes."

"And I've got—oh, twelve-fifty," Rob said, flipping through his wallet.

"Jeez, only a hundred and fifty-something—remind me never to run away with you guys again," Lewis said.

"It's not even enough to buy bus tickets—and then we have to eat," Rob said. "And it's not as if we have just one destination—we've got to *look* for the place, so we don't really know where we're going. Gabriel, how much—"

Gabriel had been shifting where he sat, noticeably impatient. "I've got about ninety dollars," he said shortly—without, Kait noticed, mentioning that he'd gotten it from Joyce's purse. "But we don't need bus tickets," he added. "I've taken care of it. We've got transportation."

"Huh?"

Gabriel shrugged and stood, brushing crumbs of dirt off his clothes. "I've got us a car. I hotwired it and it's ready. So if you're finished talking . . ."

Kaitlyn leaned her head into her hands. "Oh, God." She could *feel* the golden-white blaze of anger beside her. And now Rob was standing, moving up to get right in Gabriel's face. He was absolutely furious.

"You did *what?*" he said.

4

Gabriel gave one of his wildest smiles. "I stole us a car. What about it?"

"What about it? It's *wrong,* that's what. We are not going around stealing people's cars."

"We stole Joyce's," Gabriel said musically and mockingly.

"Joyce was trying to *kill* us. That makes it—not right, maybe, but justifiable." He got even closer to Gabriel and said with deadly anger, emphasizing each word, "There is *no* justification for stealing things from innocent people."

Gabriel was clearly enjoying himself, relaxed but ready for action any minute. He wanted to fight, Kaitlyn realized—he was dying for it. Almost as if he were feeding off the blazing energy Rob radiated. "What's *your* idea, country boy? How do we get out of here?" he said.

"I don't know, but we don't steal. It's wrong. That's

all." And for Rob, it *was* all, Kaitlyn knew. It was that simple for him.

She was chewing her lips, uneasily aware that it wasn't so simple for her. Half of her was impressed that Gabriel had gotten a car, and she had a sneaking feeling she'd be happy to ride away in it if she weren't nervous that they'd get caught. A car would be something to hold on to, an anchor against the uprooted, drifting feeling of being homeless.

But Rob would never go for it. Dear Rob. Dear honorable Rob, who was completely and utterly pigheaded and who could be the most exasperating boy on earth. Who was now glaring at Gabriel challengingly.

Gabriel bared his teeth in response. "And what about the old man? You don't think he's going to give up, do you? He'll have the police after us—and maybe other people. He has a lot of friends, a lot of connections."

It was true. Kaitlyn remembered the papers she had seen in Mr. Z's hidden room. There had been letters from judges, CEOs of big companies, people in the government. Lists of names of important people.

"We need to get out of here—*now*," Gabriel said. "And that means we need transportation." His eyes were locked on Rob's. Neither of them willing to give in.

They're going to fight, Kaitlyn thought, and she looked at Anna in despair. Anna had paused in the middle of brushing the dark and shining raven wing of her hair. She looked back worriedly at Kait.

We've got to stop them, she said.

I know, Kait thought back. *But how?*

Come up with another solution.

Kaitlyn couldn't think of another solution—and then it came to her.

Marisol, she thought.

Marisol. The research assistant back at the Institute. She'd been with Mr. Zetes even before Joyce, and she'd known about his plans. She'd tried to warn Kaitlyn—and Mr. Z had put her in a coma for it.

Kait said it aloud, with mounting excitement. "Marisol!"

It broke into Rob and Gabriel's stareout. "What?" Rob said.

Kaitlyn scrambled to her feet. "Don't you see—if anybody would help us, if anybody would believe us—and we're in *Oakland.* I'm sure Joyce said she was from Oakland."

"Kait, calm down. What are you—"

"I'm saying we should go to Marisol's *family.* They live here in Oakland. We could probably walk. And they might help us, Rob. They might understand this whole horrible thing."

The others were staring at Kait—but it was a good staring, full of dawning wonder.

"You know, they might, at that," Rob said.

"Marisol may even have told them something about it—maybe not in detail, but she might have given hints. She liked to give hints," Kait said, remembering. "And they've got to be upset over what happened. Their daughter's fine, a little moody but perfectly healthy—and then one day she falls down in a coma. Don't you think they'd have their suspicions?"

"It depends," Gabriel said. He looked dark and cold—cheated of his confrontation. "If she was taking drugs—"

"Joyce said she was taking drugs. And personally, I'm not inclined to trust anything Joyce said—are you?" Kaitlyn tilted her chin at him and to her surprise got a flash of amusement from the gray, chill eyes.

"Anyway, it's the best chance we've got," Lewis said. Always quick to see the bright side of things, he was smiling now, his dark eyes sparkling. "It's someplace to go—and maybe they'll *feed* us."

Anna twisted her hair into a long tail and stood gracefully, and Kaitlyn realized it was settled. Two minutes later they were walking down the sidewalk, looking for a phone book. Kaitlyn felt unkempt and empty—she hadn't eaten since lunch yesterday—but surprisingly fit.

The street was deserted, now, and although the fenced-in buildings were just as decrepit, the whole place looked a little safer. Lewis was cheerful enough to pull out his camera and take a picture.

"For posterity," he said.

"Maybe it's better not to look like a tourist," Anna suggested in her gentle voice.

"If anybody comes near us I'll take care of them," said Gabriel. His thoughts were still black with jagged red streaks—leftover from his fight with Rob.

Kait looked at him. "You know, I was meaning to ask you. Mr. Z said you couldn't link with another mind once you were in a stable link with us—but you linked with that policeman, and with Mr. Z and Joyce earlier."

Gabriel shrugged. "The old man was wrong," he said briefly.

Again, Kaitlyn felt a whisper of anxiety in her blood. Gabriel was hiding something from all of them. Only Gabriel, she thought, could manage that so easily in the web.

And despite his barriers, she could sense something —strange—in him. Something that had changed in the last night.

The crystal, she thought. Mr. Zetes had forced Gabriel into contact with a giant crystal, a monstrosity of jagged edges that housed unthinkable psychic power.

What if it had done something to Gabriel? Something . . . permanent?

"Gabriel," she said abruptly, "how's your forehead?"

He put his fingers to it quickly, then, deliberately, dropped his hand to his side. "Fine," he said. "Why?"

"I just wanted to look at it." Before he could stop her, she reached up herself, brushing his dark hair aside. And there on his forehead she could see it, shadowy on the pale skin. Not the kind of scab she would have expected from the cut the crystal had given him. It looked more like a scar or a birthmark—a crescent-shaped dimness.

"Right over your third eye," Kaitlyn said involuntarily, just as Gabriel grabbed her wrist in a bruising grip. She and he had both stopped dead. He stared at her, and there was something frightening in his gray gaze. Something menacing and alien that she'd never seen before.

The third eye—the seat of psychic power. And

Gabriel's powers had been greater ever since his contact with the crystal. . . .

He'd always been the strongest of all of them, psychically. It scared Kait to think what he might become if he got any stronger.

"What's *wrong* with you guys?" Lewis was demanding. The others were far ahead. Rob was walking back toward them, his brows drawn together.

Then Anna, who was farthest down the street, called, "I see a phone!"

Gabriel released Kait's wrist, almost throwing it, and started toward Anna briskly.

Leave it alone, Kaitlyn told herself. For now. For now, concentrate on surviving.

They found Marisol's name among a flood of Diazes in the phone book. Lewis wasn't familiar with Ironwood Boulevard, the street where she lived, but they studied a map at a gas station.

It was almost nine-thirty before they arrived, and Kaitlyn was hot, dusty, and starving. It was what Lewis called a pueblo house, a fake adobe house covered with pinky-brown stucco. No one answered the doorbell.

"They're not home," Kaitlyn said in despair. "I was stupid. They're at the hospital with Marisol; Joyce said they went every day."

"We'll wait. Or come back," Rob said firmly, his resolution and his temper undisturbed. They were heading toward the shade of the garage when a boy, a little older than they were, came around from the back of the house.

He had no shirt and his thin, sinewy body looked

tough. Kait would never have dared approach him on the street. But he also had curly hair that shone in the morning light like mahogany, and a full, rather sullen mouth.

In other words, thought Kaitlyn, he looks like Marisol.

For several heartbeats they all just stared at each other, the boy obviously resenting these intruders on his property, ready to fight them off. Rob and Gabriel were reacting by bristling. Then Kaitlyn stepped forward impulsively.

"Don't think we're crazy," she said. "But we're friends of Marisol's and we've run away from Mr. Zetes and we don't know where else to go. We've been on the road since last night and it took us hours to walk here. And—well, we thought you might help us."

The boy stared harder, through narrowed eyes that had long, dark lashes. Finally he said slowly, "Friends of Marisol's?"

"Yes," Kaitlyn said firmly, tucking away in her mind all the memories of how Marisol had snubbed her and terrorized her. That didn't matter now.

The boy looked each of them over, his expression sour. Just when Kaitlyn was convinced he was going to tell them to go away, he jerked his chin toward the house.

"Come on in. I'm Tony. Marisol's brother."

At the door he asked casually, "You a *bruja?* A witch?" He was looking at her eyes.

"No. I can do—things. I draw pictures and eventually they come true."

41

He nodded, still casual. Kaitlyn was vastly grateful that he seemed to believe her. He accepted the idea of psychic powers without surprise.

And despite his surly looks, he was—thoughtful. Generous. One minute after they were in the house he rubbed his chin, cast a sideways glance at Lewis, and muttered, "You been on the road, huh? You guys hungry? I was going to eat breakfast."

A lie, Kaitlyn thought. He must have seen how Lewis was sniffing at a lingering aroma of eggs and bacon. She warmed to him immediately.

"There's a lot of stuff people brought over when Marisol got sick," he said, leading them into the kitchen. From the refrigerator he pulled out a giant baking dish full of what looked like corn husks and a smaller one full of noodles. "Tamales," he said hefting the big one. He put down the small one. "And chow mein."

Fifteen minutes later they were all seated around the big kitchen table, and Kait was finishing up the story of their flight from the Institute. She told how Joyce had recruited them, how they'd come to California, how Marisol had warned them that things at the Institute weren't what they seemed, and how Mr. Zetes had finally revealed himself last night.

"He's completely evil," she said finally and looked at Tony uncertainly. But again he seemed unsurprised, merely grunting. Rob had his pile of folders and papers ready as proof, but it didn't seem necessary.

Staring down into a tamale, Kaitlyn asked the others, *Now how do we tell him Mr. Zetes put his sister in a coma?*

From every one of them—except Gabriel—she felt discomfort. Gabriel was toying with his food, apparently not interested in eating. He sat a little away from the rest of them, as usual, and looked as if he were farther away mentally.

Anna spoke up. "How is Marisol?"

"The same. The doctors say she's always going to be the same."

"We're sorry," Lewis said, wiggling his fork inside a corn husk.

"Did you ever think," Rob said quietly, "that there was anything—strange—about what happened to her?"

Tony looked at him directly. "Everything was strange. Marisol didn't take drugs. I heard some stuff last week about how she was supposed to be on medication—but it wasn't true."

"Joyce Piper told *us* she was on medication. She told us Marisol was seeing a psychiatrist. . . ." Rob's voice trailed off, because Tony was shaking his head vigorously. "Not true?"

"She saw a shrink once or twice last year, because of the really weird stuff that was going on. That was when she worked at Zetes's house. He had some sick people there—for a study, Marisol said."

"The pilot study? You know about that?" Kaitlyn leaned forward eagerly. "Marisol mentioned it—a study with other psychics like the one Mr. Zetes was doing with us."

Rob was sorting through the folders, pulling out one Kaitlyn had seen before. It was a file jacket with a photo of a brown-haired girl labeled SABRINA JESSICA GALLO, BLACK LIGHTNING PILOT STUDY.

Scrawled across the label in thick red ink was the word TERMINATED.

Tony was nodding. "Bri Gallo. She was one of them. I think they had six all together. They were into some really bizarre crap. Sick. Zetes had this mental domination over them."

He shifted, seemed to consider, then said, "I'll tell you a story. There was a guy who worked with Marisol, another assistant. He didn't like the boss, thought Zetes was crazy. He used to fight, you know? Talk back. Show up late. And finally he decided he was going to talk to a newspaper about what was going on at that house. He told Marisol that one night. She said the next morning when she saw him, he was— different. He didn't talk back anymore, and he sure didn't talk about any newspapers. He just did his work like he was sleepwalking. Like somebody *enbrujado*—under a spell."

"A spell?" Kait wondered. "Or drugs?"

"Stranger than drugs. He kept on working there, and he kept on getting paler and sleepier. Marisol said he had this blank look, like he was there but his soul wasn't." Tony glanced toward the hallway where a large candle burned in a niche beneath a statue of the Virgin Mary. Simply and unemotionally he said, "I think Boss Zetes works black magic."

Kaitlyn glanced at Rob, who was listening intently, his eyes amber-brown and grim. He met her gaze and said silently, *It's as good a word as any for what he does with that crystal. And maybe Mr. Z does have some mental powers we don't know about.*

Aloud, Kaitlyn said, "He used drugs on Marisol.

Joyce Piper gave her something—I don't know what, but I saw it in a vision."

At first Tony seemed not to have heard. He said, "I told her to get out. A long time ago. But she was ambitious, you know? She made money, she bought a car, she was going to get her own place. She said she could handle things."

Kaitlyn, who had always been poor, could understand that.

"She did try to get out in the end," Rob said. "Or at least to get us out. And that was why Mr. Z had to stop her."

Tony grabbed a kitchen knife and slammed it into the wooden table.

Kait's heart almost jumped out of her body. Anna froze, her dark owl eyes on Tony's face. Lewis winced, and Rob frowned.

Gabriel, his eyes on the quivering knife handle, smiled.

"Lo siento," Tony muttered. "I'm sorry. But he shouldn't have done that to Marisol."

Almost without thinking, Kaitlyn put her hand on his. Back in Ohio she would have laughed at the idea. She'd hated boys, loud, smelly, interfering boys. But she understood exactly what Tony was feeling.

"Rob wants to stop him—Mr. Zetes," she said. "And we have this idea that if we can get to this certain place, we might get help. There are people there who act like they're against the Institute."

"Can those people help Marisol?"

Kaitlyn had to be honest. "I don't know. But if you want, we'll ask them. I promise."

Tony nodded. He took his hand from under Kaitlyn's and wiped his eye absently.

"We're not even sure who they are," Rob said. "We think they live somewhere up north, and we have an idea of what the location looks like. We figure it may take us a while to find them, and we'll be on the road all that time. The only problem is that we don't know how to get there."

"No," Gabriel broke sarcastically, speaking for the first time since they'd arrived. "That's not the only problem. The other problem is that we're broke. And stranded."

Tony looked at him, then smiled. It was a crooked smile, but genuine, as if he liked Gabriel's directness.

"We thought we might talk to your parents," Kaitlyn said delicately. "If we go to our own parents they'll find us, you see. And our parents wouldn't understand."

Tony shook his head. He stared out the window into a neat backyard as if thinking. At last he said, "Don't wait for my parents. It'll only upset them."

"But—"

"Come on outside."

Kaitlyn and the others exchanged looks. The web was as blank with surprise as their faces. They followed.

The backyard was filled with dormant rosebushes. There was an extension of the driveway behind an iron gate. On the driveway was a silver-blue van.

"Hey, that's the van from the Institute," Lewis said.

Tony had stopped and was regarding it with folded arms. He shook his head. "No, it's Marisol's. It was hers. It is hers." He stood for a moment, shaking his head as if trying to figure this out, then turned abruptly to Kait. "You take it."

"What?"

"I'll get some stuff—sleeping bags and things. We've got an old tent in the garage."

Kaitlyn was overwhelmed. "But—"

"You need stuff for a trip, right? Otherwise you're going to dic out there. You're never going to make it." He shook off Kaitlyn's reaching hand and backed up, but he met her eyes. His voice was almost a growl. "And you're going to fight *him,* the bastard that hurt Marisol. Nobody else is. Nobody else *can,* because you need magic to fight magic. You take the van."

His eyes were Marisol's eyes, too, Kaitlyn realized. Rich brown almost the color of his hair. She could feel her own eyes filling, but she held his gaze. "Thank you," she said softly.

And we'll do whatever we can to get them to help Marisol, she thought. She knew the others could hear her, but it was really a private promise.

"We better get you out of here before my mom gets back," Tony said. He took Rob and Lewis into the garage. Kait, Anna, and Gabriel examined the van.

"It's perfect," Kaitlyn whispered, looking around the inside. She'd ridden in it before, to and from school, but she'd never really *looked* at it. To her eyes now, there seemed to be square miles of room. There were two bucket seats in front and two long bench seats in back, with lots of space between them.

There still seemed to be miles of room once Tony piled in blankets, sleeping bags, and pillows. Riches untold, Kaitlyn thought, fingering a thick down-filled comforter. He even took Gabriel and Rob back into the house and lent them spare clothes. Finally he put groceries from the refrigerator into a paper bag.

"It won't last long with five of you, but it's something," he said.

"Thank you," Kait said again as they got ready to leave. Rob was in the driver's seat; Gabriel in the other front bucket seat. Anna and Lewis were in the bench seat behind them. Kaitlyn had ended up in the rear bench seat—too far from Rob, but no matter. They'd change places later.

"You just get Zetes, right?" Tony said, then slid the door of the van shut.

We're going to try, Kaitlyn thought. She waved as Rob backed out of the driveway.

"Keep going down this street and I'll tell you how to get back on Highway 880," Lewis said. He was studying a map of California that Tony had supplied. When they were on the highway, he changed it for a map of the United States.

"Well, we've got clothes, we've got food, and we've got sleeping gear. And we certainly have transport," Rob said, settling back in his bucket seat and running a caressing hand over the steering wheel. "Now—exactly where are we going?"

5

"Let's just get out of California as fast as possible," Gabriel said. Rob wouldn't agree.

"We ought to think about this before we just start driving blindly. We're looking for a beach, right? There are a lot of beaches in California—"

"But we *know* it's not in California," Kait interrupted. "Anna and I know that. We're sure." In front of her, Anna was nodding.

"And we've got to get *out* of this state," Gabriel said. "This is where the cops will be looking for us. Once we're in Oregon we can relax a little."

Kaitlyn was afraid Rob would argue just for the sake of arguing with Gabriel—she wasn't sure how things stood between them just now—but he just shrugged and said, "Okay, then," peaceably.

Lewis rattled the map. "The fastest way is to go up Interstate 5," he said. "I'll tell you how to get there. We still won't make it to Oregon before dark."

"We can change drivers every few hours," Kaitlyn

said. "Oh, and everybody, try and look like you're on a field trip or something, at least until one o'clock or so. People might think it's strange for a bunch of teenagers to be riding around in a van during school hours."

The country kept changing as they drove. At first it was beige and flat, with scrubby grass and an occasional gray-purple bush beside the road. As they got farther north it became more hilly, with trees that were either bare or dusty green. Kait watched it all with an artist's eye and eventually picked up her sketchpad.

It felt like a long while since she'd had time to draw. It had only been twenty-four hours, since yesterday's art studio class—but her entire life of yesterday felt years away. The oil pastels spread smoothly onto the fine-toothed paper, and Kaitlyn felt herself relax. She needed this.

She blocked out the shape of the distant hills with side strokes of the pastel stick, catching an impression of them before the scene changed. That's what she liked about pastels—you could work fast on a burst of inspiration. She filled the hills in with loose, vigorous strokes, and the picture was done in minutes.

That was practice. Now turn the page. Reach for cool colors—pale blue and icy mauve. Maybe acid green and blue-purple, too.

A picture was coming alive under her fingers without her conscious intent.

Kaitlyn was used to letting her fingers go at moments like this, while her mind simply drifted. Right now her mind had drifted to thoughts of Gabriel.

She was going to have to talk with him, and soon. As

soon as she could find any privacy. Something serious was wrong. She had to find out what it was. . . .

With a shock Kaitlyn recognized what she'd drawn on the sketch pad.

Gabriel. Not the stark black-and-white portrait she'd always imagined, but a form arising out of a dense network of colored lines. It was unmistakably Gabriel . . .

. . . and in the center of his forehead, blazing with cold blue brilliance, was a third eye.

It seemed to glare at her balefully, and Kaitlyn suddenly felt faint. As if she were about to fall into the picture.

She jerked back, and the sensation disappeared, but chills ran down her neck.

Stop it, she told herself. There was nothing strange about a picture of the third eye. Gabriel was psychic, wasn't he? And this just a metaphor showing he was. She'd drawn a picture of herself with a third eye once.

The reassurances didn't reassure. Kaitlyn knew in her bones that the drawing foretold something evil.

Kait, what's wrong?

Rob's voice in her head. Kaitlyn looked up from the maze of colors to see that everyone was looking at her. Gabriel had turned around in the front, and Lewis and Anna were looking over the back of their seat. She could see Rob's worried eyes in the rearview mirror.

While she'd been drawing she'd forgotten about the web, hadn't even felt the presence of the others. And she could tell from their confusion that they hadn't heard *her* thoughts, either, just gotten a general sense that she was upset.

Interesting, one part of her mind said. So drawing is

a way to screen my thoughts. Or maybe it's just concentrating.

Meanwhile, the rest of her mind was answering Rob.

It's nothing. Just a drawing.

She felt Rob's alarm. "A precognition?" he said aloud.

"No—I don't know." It was horribly impossible to lie in the web. "Whatever it is, I don't want to talk about it now."

She didn't, either. Not with Gabriel sitting there hearing every word, not with Lewis and Anna looking on. Gabriel would be furious at the violation of his privacy, and the others might panic. No, Kaitlyn had to talk to him alone about this first.

She could feel frustration from Rob—he could tell she was hiding something, but not *what*. Anna's clear dark eyes were questioning.

Time to change the subject. "Shouldn't we stop and switch drivers?" she said.

Lewis grinned. "Let's wait a couple of exits and stop at the Olive Pit. There was a sign back there advertising free samples."

"This must be olive country," Kait said, glad of a distraction. "I keep seeing groves of olive trees."

She kept talking until they stopped, and then there was the complexity of selecting olive samples—chili olives and Cajun olives and Texas olives and Deep South olives—and by the time they all got back into the van everyone seemed to have forgotten their questions.

Gabriel drove. Rob sat in the rear with Kaitlyn, who leaned against him.

The Possessed

"You all right?" he said, too softly for the others to hear.

Kaitlyn nodded, avoiding his golden eyes. She didn't *want* to have any secrets from Rob, but she was afraid to upset the precarious balance between him and Gabriel.

"Just tired," she said. She didn't feel like drawing anymore, not even when a huge and beautiful mountain appeared before them in the distance. Its single peak was white with snow, accented by black ridges of rock.

"Mount Shasta," Lewis said.

They passed rolling hills and crossed riverbeds, mostly dry. The motion and the sound of the van was lulling. Kait's head drooped onto Rob's shoulder and her eyes shut.

She woke with a start and a shiver. How strange—it was *cold* suddenly. Icy cold, as if she'd stepped into a restaurant freezer.

She looked around, dazed with sleep. Mount Shasta was behind them, glowing like a huge watermelon jewel in the sunset. The sky was murky mauve.

In the front bench seat Anna's black head was lifting. "Gabriel, turn down the air conditioning!" she pleaded.

"It's not on."

"But it's *cold,*" Kait said and was caught by another shiver.

Shivering himself, Rob wrapped his arms around her. "It sure is," he said. "We haven't gone *that* far north—is it usually like this, Lewis?"

Lewis didn't answer. Kait saw Anna look at him

53

curiously, and at the same time realized she could sense nothing from him in the web.

"Is he asleep?" she asked Anna.

"His eyes are open."

Kaitlyn's heart rate seemed to quicken. *Lewis?* she thought, sending the word to him.

Nothing.

"What's happening?" she said aloud as Rob let go of her to lean around the front seat and look into Lewis's face. She had a bad feeling—a very bad feeling. Something was *strange*. The air wasn't just cold, it was full of electricity. And there was a smell, a smell like a sewer drain.

And a sound. Kaitlyn heard it suddenly over the soft roar of the van's engine. A sharp, sweet sound, one note, as if somebody had run a wet finger around the rim of a crystal goblet. It hung in the air.

"What the *hell* is going on?" Rob demanded. He was shaking Lewis. At the same moment Gabriel snarled from the front, "What are you guys *doing* back there?"

"We're not doing anything," Kait called—just as Lewis jumped up and dived for the empty bucket seat beside Gabriel.

His hands grabbed and beat at the air. His body slammed into Gabriel, who cursed and wrestled with the steering wheel. The van swerved.

"Get out of here! Get him out of here!" Gabriel shouted. "I can't see—"

Rob twisted in behind Lewis, trying to pull him back. The van kept swerving and skidding as Lewis's elbows hit Gabriel. Kaitlyn clung to the seat in front of her, frozen.

"Come *on!*" Rob yelled. *Lewis, come on back! There's nothing there!*

Lewis kept on fighting, and then all at once he went limp, and like a cork popping out of a bottle, he shot backward with Rob. They both crashed into Anna, who yelped. Then they fell in a tangle on the floor.

"Hey—what's the matter? You getting fresh or something?" Lewis said. "Let go of me."

It was an ordinary, complaining voice. Lewis was disentangling himself, looking mildly bewildered but absolutely normal.

Rob sat up and stared at him.

Gabriel had finally gotten the van on course again. He shot a glare over his shoulder. "You crazy jerk," he said. "What'd you think you were doing?"

"Me? I wasn't doing anything. Rob was grabbing me." Lewis looked around at all of them, his round face honestly puzzled.

"Lewis—you really don't remember?" Kaitlyn asked. She could tell by his expression, by his presence in the web that he didn't. "You jumped up and started beating on something in that seat," she said, nodding. "Only there was nothing there."

"Oh . . ." A sort of light was dawning on Lewis's face. Then his expression turned sheepish. "I guess—I was dreaming, you know? I don't really remember the dream, but I thought I saw somebody sitting there. A kind of whitish shape—a person. And I knew I had to get it. . . ." His voice trailed off. He gave another look around and hunched his shoulders apologetically.

"A dream," Gabriel said in disgust. "Next time keep your dreams to yourself."

A dream? Kaitlyn thought. No. It didn't make sense; it couldn't be the whole explanation. Why should Lewis suddenly start having dreams that made him attack things? And what about the cold—it had disappeared as quickly as it had come; the air felt fine now. And the drain smell, and that sound . . .

We're all tired, Anna's gentle voice said in her head, reminding her that she hadn't been trying to shield her thoughts. *Not just tired but exhausted. And we've been under so much stress—it could come out in strange ways.*

"We could all have been dreaming a little," Rob said with a laugh.

"I suppose," Kaitlyn said. She tried to put any further doubts out of her mind—for now, at least. Lewis obviously believed his own story, and Anna and Rob believed him because he believed it. There was no point in harping on it.

We'll wait and see what happens, she told herself. She settled back on the seat, and Rob returned to sit by her again. The light was fading in a way that made her want to check if she was wearing sunglasses. To the west and in front of them were huge flaming hot cherry clouds.

"Should we stop?" Rob asked, peering at his watch in the dimness.

Gabriel turned the van's headlights on. "We're still in California. We can stop when we get to Oregon."

The sky went gray and then black. Ghost trucks with dazzling headlights came and went on the other side of the highway. It was nearly eight o'clock when they reached a sign saying WELCOME TO OREGON.

They drove on until they found a rest stop and then

ate dinner sitting on the cool dark grass outside the van. Dinner was peanut butter sandwiches and one apple apiece, drawn from the grocery bag Tony had given them. Dessert was some cherry cough drops Lewis had found in the glove compartment and the last of the Cajun olive samples.

"We can stay here tonight," Rob said, looking around the almost-deserted rest stop. There were few cars on the highway nearby. "Nobody will bother us."

Kait found she'd brought toothpaste but no toothbrush. In the women's rest room she rubbed her teeth with a corner of a cotton shirt she'd packed. They all wanted to go to bed early.

"But *how?*" Kaitlyn said when she got back, confronted at last with the logistics of five of them sleeping in the van. Suddenly there no longer seemed to be acres of room. "Where do we all *fit?*"

"The rear seat reclines," Rob said. He and Lewis had the back of the van open and were fiddling with the bench seats. "See, it folds back into a flat bed. That's room for two people there. Somebody else can sleep on the other bench seat, and then the two bucket seats in front recline."

"I'll take one of those," Lewis said. "Unless somebody wants to share the back . . . ?" He looked from Anna to Kait hopefully.

"The girls can have the back," Rob said.

Anna's dark eyes were laughing. "Oh, no . . . I think you and Kaitlyn should have the back. I'll sleep on the other bench."

"And *I'll* sleep outside," Gabriel said shortly, leaning in from the front and yanking a sleeping bag out of the pile.

Daggers and broken glass, that was what Kait felt from him through the web. She and Rob hadn't even *agreed* yet, although she knew they would. She liked to sleep close to Rob, it felt safe. And she knew Rob liked to have her close, because then he didn't worry about her as much.

"It's just convenience," she began, but Gabriel cut her off with a look. He seemed pale and tense under the van's interior lights.

"Look, I don't think it's such a good idea, sleeping outside," Rob said in a mild voice. Gabriel gave him the look, too.

"I can take care of myself," he said and showed his teeth.

He left the van. Kaitlyn helped Rob spread out blankets automatically, trying to screen her thoughts from the others. She still hadn't had a chance to speak to Gabriel privately. She was going to have to *make* a chance, and soon.

Sleeping in the back of the van was cramped and a little stuffy—like sleeping in a compartment on a train, Kaitlyn guessed. But she didn't really mind being crowded in with Rob. He was warm and nice to hang on to. Comfortingly solid.

It was the first time they had been alone together— and Kaitlyn was so tired her eyelids felt like lead weights. There were no golden sparks at his touch now, just a steady shining light that seemed to pour reassurance into her.

"I love you," she murmured sleepily, and they kissed. A sweet kiss that made her cling to him afterward.

I love you, Rob thought back. His thought carried

the essence of *him* with it—pure Rob. Warm as sunlight, with an underlying hint of strength that made Kait think of lions basking in the savanna. Rob had a fine stubborn temper of his own, but he cared too much about other people to let it rule him.

And he didn't care who heard him say he loved her. A vocal whisper would have been much more private than telepathy. Distantly Kaitlyn could feel tolerant amusement laced with envy from Lewis and peaceful approval from Anna—but from outside the van, from Gabriel, a wave of dark repudiation. Bitterness. An anger that frightened her.

He feels that he's been cheated of something, she thought, even as she clung harder to Rob. But that's not right; I never led him on. . . .

We've got to find a way to break this link, Rob said stiffly. *It's all right when you want it, but having people spying on your thoughts when you don't want—*

"Rob, don't annoy him," Kait whispered. Rob was broadcasting loud and clear, and Gabriel was getting angrier by the minute. The two of them together were like flint and iron—sparking off each other at every opportunity.

I've said from the beginning that we've got to get rid of it, Gabriel said from outside. *And I know of one certain way, at least.*

He meant for one of them to die. It had come to that, Gabriel threatening them again, acting as if he hated them all.

"Leave it alone," Kaitlyn hissed before Rob could answer. "Oh, *please,* Rob, just leave it; I'm so tired." To her surprise she felt on the verge of tears.

Rob immediately gave up the argument, mentally

turning his back on Gabriel. *We'll find a way to break it—another way,* he promised Kaitlyn. *The people in the white house will help us. And if they don't, I'll find a way.*

"Yes," Kaitlyn murmured, her eyes shutting. Rob was holding her close, and she believed him, as she'd believed in him from the beginning. She couldn't help it; Rob *made* you believe.

"Go to sleep, Kait," he whispered, and Kaitlyn sank into the darkness fearlessly.

As long as you're with me I'm not afraid, she thought.

The last thing she heard before sleep was a distant whisper from Anna. "I wonder if we'll dream again?"

Gabriel twisted inside the sleeping bag. There was nothing but grass underneath him, but he felt as if he were lying on roots—or bones.

Ghoulish thought. The bones of the dead beneath him. Maybe the bones of his personal dead, the ones he'd dispatched himself. That would be poetic justice, at least.

Though he wouldn't have admitted it to anyone, Gabriel believed in justice.

Not that he regretted having killed the guy in Stockton. The one who'd been ready to shoot him over the five crumpled dollar bills in his jeans pocket. He was quite happy to have sent that particular home boy to hell.

But that had been his second murder. The first had been unintentional—the product of what happened when a strong mind came in contact with a weaker one. He'd been strong, and Iris—sweet Iris—had been weak. Fragile as a little white mouse, delicate as a flower. Her life energy had poured into him as if one of her arteries had been cut. And he—

—hadn't been able to stop it.

Not until it was over and she was lying limp and motionless in his arms. Her face blue-white. Her lips parted.

Gabriel found that he was lying rigid, staring straight up into the endless darkness of the night sky. His hands were clenched into fists and he was sweating.

I'd die if it would bring her back, he thought with sudden clarity. I'd change places with her. I belong in hell with home boy, but Iris belongs here.

It was strange, but he couldn't really remember her face anymore. He could remember loving her, but not what she'd looked like alive, except that her gaze had been wide-open and defenseless, like a deer's.

And he couldn't take her place. Things weren't that *simple* in the universe; he wasn't going to get off that easy. No, his part was to lie here on grass that felt like bones and think about the new murders, the ones that he was going to commit, inevitably, in the future.

There wasn't any other way for him.

The girl in Oakland—that scrawny ratbag with the tattoo—he hadn't killed her, quite. He'd left her in an alley with her life force almost drained, but still flowing. She'd live.

But tonight . . . the need was stronger. Gabriel hadn't expected that. He'd been feeling it for hours, the parched, cracked-earth sensation, and by now it was almost unbearable. It was all he could do not to rip into Kessler, who was a constant beacon of energy, radiating it like a lighthouse or one of those stars that flared regularly. The temptation was almost unendurable, especially when Kessler was being annoying, which was almost always.

No. He couldn't touch any of his own group. Aside from the fact that it would blow his secret, it was— impolite. Impolitic. Uncivil.

And wrong, the distant part of his mind whispered.

Shut up, Gabriel told it.

He was out of his sleeping bag in one lithe twist.

Since Rob the Wonder Boy was off limits, he would have to go hunting elsewhere. Through the web, Gabriel could feel the deep sleep of his mind-mates; through the windows of the van he saw nothing. Nobody was going to miss him.

He looked around under the stars for someone to quench his thirst.

6

The people were leaning over her. The first thing Kait noticed was that they looked like pencil drawings —monochrome, all the color sucked out. The second thing was that they were evil.

She didn't know how she knew that, but it was clear. Clearer than the faces of the people. It wasn't that they didn't have features, but the features seemed blurred, as if they were moving back and forth thousands of times a second, or as if something about them had affected Kait's sight.

Aliens, she thought wildly. Little gray people from flying saucers. And then: Lewis's white shape.

Kaitlyn's heart began pounding with deep sick thuds that seemed to choke off her breath.

She wanted to scream, but that was impossible. She didn't even know if she were awake or asleep, but she was paralyzed.

If I could move—if I could just move I could tell. I could make them go away. . . .

What she wanted to do was to kick upward with her legs and lash out with her arms to see if the visions were solid. But she couldn't even lift her knee. The things were leaning over her from all sides. There was a strange property about them—when Kaitlyn looked at any one of them, it seemed to be rushing toward her, but the group stayed in the same place. They were *looking* at her. Staring with a fixed blank gaze that was worse than any malevolence. And they seemed to be bending farther down, coming closer . . .

With a violent jerk Kaitlyn managed to lift her arm. At least, it felt like a violent jerk to her, but what she saw was her arm rising feebly and almost dreamily toward the figures. It brushed through one monochrome leaning face, and she felt a shock of coldness on the skin.

Refrigerated air . . .

The figures were gone.

Kait lay on her back, blinking. Her eyes were open now, and she thought they'd been open the whole while—but how could she tell? She was staring into darkness as black as the blackness behind closed lids. The only thing she could see was the faint shape of her arm waving in the cold air.

Cold—the air was definitely cold. And there had been a sudden drop in temperature just before Lewis saw *his* vision.

I don't believe it was a dream, Kaitlyn thought. Or not an ordinary dream.

But then, what? A premonition? She didn't have premonitions that way, and Lewis didn't have them at all. Lewis had psychokinesis, PK, the power to move objects with his mind.

Whatever it had been, it had left her with a terrible sick feeling. There was a—a *running* in her middle, a hot restless feeling that made it agony to lie still. She felt cramped and her eyes ached and her whole body was vibrating with adrenaline.

Rob was lying peacefully beside her, his breathing even. Deeply asleep. Kaitlyn hated to wake him; he needed the rest. Lewis and Anna were sleeping soundly, too—she could feel that through the web.

And Gabriel outside? Kait sent her mind searching, doing something she couldn't have described to an outsider. It was like wondering how your foot was feeling, concentrating your attention on a particular part of yourself in a particular location. Somehow she could wonder how Gabriel was doing, and then feel . . .

. . . that he wasn't there, she realized with a shock. Not outside the van where he had been before. She could sense him dimly—somewhere else—but she couldn't locate him exactly, and she couldn't tell what he was doing.

Fine. *Good.* With sudden determination Kaitlyn inched her legs up, pulling the blanket off her by degrees. Just as slowly, she sat up and then stood, crouching, edging sideways to the door in the middle of the van.

She passed Anna, curled neatly on her short bench, black hair swathing her face. Lewis's bucket seat was reclined so far she had to reach under it to get the door open. But finally, with a clank, the door slid back.

Kaitlyn could feel everyone stir, then settle again. She dropped lightly out of the van and shut the door as quietly as she could.

Now. She was going to find Gabriel. Her nervous energy would be put to good use—she was going to *talk* to him, confront him about the strangeness she'd felt inside him, about what he'd been doing when he'd left them all last night. It was the perfect opportunity; with the others asleep, they'd have complete privacy. And if Gabriel didn't like it—tough. Kaitlyn was wound up and ready for a fight herself.

She turned from the van and looked around the rest stop. Aside from the lighted bulk of the rest rooms, everything was dark. There were only three cars to be seen—a battered Volkswagen Bug, a lowslung Chevy, and a white Cadillac.

And no Gabriel. Kaitlyn couldn't get a location on him. She peered into the darkness behind and in front of her, then shrugged and started walking.

He was here *somewhere*. Just walled off so she couldn't feel him. As if he lived in a private fortress. Well, she'd explain differently to him; he was *part* of them, and he couldn't keep denying it.

And he shouldn't be wandering around alone like this in the dark. Kait passed the Bug and the Chevy, noting absently that Oregon license plates had pictures of mountains on them. She passed the Cadillac, which was parked under the last streetlight, and hesitated on the brink of the darkness beyond.

That way . . . she had an urge to go that way. An instinct. If there was one thing Kait had learned recently, it was to trust her instincts—but it was lonely-looking out there, lit only by a half-full moon just beginning to rise.

Bracing herself, she began to move cautiously forward, stepping off the sidewalk onto grass. The ground curved down, leading toward a lonely clump of trees—Kait could see their upper branches against the lighter black of the night sky.

It was very quiet, and Kaitlyn's skin was prickling, tiny hairs lifting. Well, that wasn't surprising: Oregon was cooler than California. It was just the night air.

But where *was* Gabriel? Kaitlyn was moving blindly toward the trees, but it wasn't like Gabriel to go sit under a tree. Maybe instinct had been wrong this time.

All right, she'd go just down to that first tree—she could see it fairly well now that her eyes were adjusting to the darkness—and then she'd turn back. She was far enough from the van that she could only feel Rob and Lewis and Anna very dimly, and she knew that communication would be impossible.

I'm truly alone, she thought. The only way any of us can be alone now, by getting out of range of the others. Maybe that's why Gabriel's been wandering off at night; I could understand that. Simply to get some distance.

She almost had herself convinced by the time she got to the tree.

What she found there she discovered with all her senses at once. Her ears picked up some slight sound of movement and the hiss of a ragged breath. Her eyes made out a shape half concealed behind the tree. And her psychic senses felt a disturbance in the web—a *shimmering,* as if she'd stepped near a charged field.

All the same, she could hardly make herself believe what she was witnessing. Heart beating madly, she stepped closer, moving around the tree. The shape— in the moonlight it looked like a romantic painting of

Romeo and Juliet, a kneeling boy holding a limp girl in his arms. But the sound, the quick panting breath —that was more like an animal.

What she felt through the web was animalistic, too. It was hunger.

Please, no, Kaitlyn thought. She'd begun to shake, an uncontrollable trembling that started in her legs and went everywhere. Please, God, I don't want to see this. . . .

But then the kneeling boy raised his head, and there was no way to deny it anymore.

Gabriel. It was Gabriel and he was holding a girl who looked unconscious or dead, and when he looked up, it was straight into Kaitlyn's eyes.

She could see the shock on his face—and in the web she felt a shattering. A crashing-down of walls as the barriers he'd been holding around himself collapsed. She'd taken him off guard, and suddenly she could feel—everything.

Everything he was going through. Everything he was experiencing at that moment.

"Gabriel—" she gasped aloud.

Hunger, she got back. She could feel it pounding at her. Hunger and desperation. An intolerable, agonizing pain—and the promise of relief in the girl he was holding. A girl who wasn't dead, Kaitlyn realized, but comatose and bursting with life energy. What Lewis called *chi.*

"Gabriel," Kaitlyn said again. Her legs were wobbling; they weren't going to support her much longer. She was overwhelmed by the need she felt—*his* need.

"Get away," Gabriel said hoarsely.

She was surprised he could talk. There wasn't much

rationality in his presence in the web. What Kait felt there seemed less like Gabriel than some shark or starving wolf. A desperate, merciless hunter ready to make his kill.

Run, something inside Kaitlyn said. He's about to kill, and it could be you as easily as that girl. Be smart and *run* . . .

"Gabriel, listen to me. I won't hurt you." Kaitlyn got the words out raggedly, on separate breaths, but she managed to hold her hands out toward him almost steadily. "Gabriel, I understand—I can *feel* what you need. But there has to be another way."

"Get *out* of here," Gabriel snarled.

Ignoring the terrified sickness in her stomach, Kaitlyn took a step toward him. Think, she was telling herself frantically. Think, be rational—because *he* certainly isn't.

Gabriel's lips peeled back from his teeth, and he jerked the girl to him. As if protecting his prey from an intruder. "Don't come any closer," he hissed.

"It's energy, isn't it?" Kaitlyn didn't dare take another step, so she dropped to her knees instead. She was at Gabriel's level now, and she could see that his eyes were like two windows opening on darkness. "It's life energy you need. I can feel that. I can feel how much it hurts—"

"You can't feel anything! Get out before you really do get hurt!" It was a tortured cry, but almost instantly afterward Gabriel stilled. A deathly calm spread over his face, and his eyes went like black ice. Kaitlyn could feel his purposefulness in the web.

Without looking at her, ignoring her completely, he turned his attention to the girl in his arms. The girl had soft curly hair—dark blond or light brown, Kaitlyn thought. She looked almost peaceful. Gabriel had undoubtedly stunned her with his mind somehow.

Now he turned her head to one side, pushing the disordered curls off the back of her neck. Kaitlyn watched in horror, frozen by the cool deliberation of his movements.

"Right here," Gabriel whispered, and he touched the nape of the girl's neck, a point at the upper part of the spine, just between vertebrae. "This is the transfer point. The best place to take energy. You can stay and watch if you want."

His voice was like an Arctic wind, and his presence in the web like ice. He was looking at the girl's neck with cold hunger, eyes narrowed, lips skinned back a little.

And then, as Kaitlyn watched, he bent to put his lips to the girl's skin.

"No!"

Kait didn't know what she was going to do until she did it. But suddenly she was moving, she was throwing herself across the little distance to Gabriel. She was putting her hands between the girl and him—one hand on the girl's neck, the other on Gabriel's face. She felt his lips, and then the brush of teeth.

Keep out of this! Gabriel's mental shout was so powerful it sent shockwaves through Kaitlyn. But she hung on.

Give her to me! he shouted. Kaitlyn's vision was red; she could see nothing, feel nothing, but the all-encompassing fury of Gabriel's hunger. He was a snarling, clawing animal now—and she was fighting him.

And losing. She was weaker, both physically and psychically, and he was utterly ruthless. He was tearing the girl away from her, his mind a black hole ready to consume. . . .

No, Gabriel, Kaitlyn thought—and she kissed him.

That was the result, anyway, of her sudden darting movement. She'd meant for a different contact—forehead to forehead, the way Rob had touched her to channel healing energy once. But at the touch of his lips against hers she felt a shock of a different sort and it was an instant before she could pull back to get the position right.

She'd shocked Gabriel, too—shocked him into stillness. He seemed too astonished to fight her or jerk away. He simply sat, paralyzed, as Kaitlyn shut her eyes, and, gripping his shoulders, thrust her forehead against his.

Oh.

That simple contact, skin to skin, third eye to third eye, brought the biggest shock of all. A jolt that went through Kait like lightning—as if two ends of electric wiring had touched, sending a violent current coursing through.

Oh, she thought. *Oh . . .*

It was frightening—terrifying in its power. And for the first instant it hurt. She felt a tearing in her body, in her bloodstream—as if something was being pulled out of her. A vital pain at the roots of her being. Dimly, with some part of her mind that could still think, she remembered what Gabriel had said once.

That people were afraid he would steal their souls. That was what this felt like.

And yet, at the same time, it was compelling. It swept her along with it, helpless to resist. It demanded that she surrender. . . .

You wanted to help him, the part of Kait that could still think said. So help him. *Give.* Give what he needs.

Kaitlyn felt a wrenching—and then a bursting. It was as if some barrier in her had been broken, ripping under pressure. She trembled violently—and felt herself *give.*

It still hurt, but in a new way. A strange way that was almost pleasure. Like the release of something painful, blocked . . . backed-up.

Kait had received psychic energy before, taking Rob's healing power when she'd been drained and exhausted. But she'd never given it, not on this scale. Now she felt a torrent of energy flowing from her into Gabriel, like a flood of golden sparks. And she could feel him responding, drinking in the energy greedily, gratefully. The darkness inside him, the black hole, being lit up by the gold.

Life, Kaitlyn thought dizzily. It's life I'm giving him really. He needs this or he'll die.

And then: Is this how healers feel? Oh, no wonder Rob likes doing it. There's nothing like it, nothing . . . especially if you *want* to help.

For the most part, though, she couldn't think at all. She simply *experienced,* feeling Gabriel's hunger gradually being sated, the burning need in him slowly cooling as it was met. And feeling his amazement, his wonder.

He was less of an animal now, and more Gabriel.

72

The Gabriel who had tried to protect her from the pain of Mr. Zetes's great crystal, the Gabriel who'd had tears in his eyes when he spoke of his past. Kaitlyn realized suddenly that she'd gotten behind his walls again. She was seeing, touching, the Gabriel that was kept hidden from the world.

It's different—like this. The thought was almost a whisper, but it shook Kaitlyn with its strength. Its— intensity. She could feel the astonished gratitude behind it, and something like awe. *Different . . . when I took energy before—when I took it last night—it wasn't like this.*

And because Gabriel's mind was open to her, Kait knew what he meant. She could *see* the girl from last night, the one with the straggly hair and the unicorn tattoo. And she could taste the girl's fear, her anguish and aversion.

She was unwilling, Kaitlyn told Gabriel. *You forced her; she didn't want to help you. I do.*

Why?

One word, with the force of a blow behind it. Kaitlyn felt Gabriel's hands tighten on her shoulders as he projected the thought. She hadn't been aware of her physical body for some time, but now she realized that she and Gabriel were clinging to each other, still in contact at the transfer point. The curly-haired girl, the new victim, had fallen or been shoved aside.

Why? Gabriel repeated, almost brutally, demanding an answer.

Because I care about you! Kaitlyn shot back. The violence of the first channeling of energy was gone, but she could still feel it flowing from herself to him. And she could feel, in some distant way, an approach-

73

ing dizziness, a weakness. She ignored it. *Because I care what happens to you, because I—*

Abruptly, with no warning at all, Gabriel pulled away. Whatever Kaitlyn had been about to say was lost.

The jolt of broken contact was almost as bad as the moment of initiation. Kaitlyn's eyes flew open. She could see the world again, but she felt blind. Blind and horribly alone. Even feeling Gabriel in the web was nothing to the intimacy of direct energy transfer.

Gabriel . . .

"It's enough," he said, speaking instead of returning her thought. She could feel him trying to gather his walls again. "I'm all right now. You did what you meant to do."

"Gabriel," Kaitlyn said. There was a terrible wistfulness inside her. Without thinking, she raised a hand to touch his face.

Gabriel flinched back.

Hurt and loss flooded over Kait. She clamped her lips together.

"Don't," Gabriel said. Then he looked away, shaking his head. "I'm not trying to hurt you, damn it!" he said sharply. "It's just—don't you realize how dangerous that was? I could have drained you. I could have killed you." He turned back and looked directly into her eyes again, with a sudden fierceness that frightened Kaitlyn. *"I could have killed you,"* he repeated with vicious emphasis.

"You didn't. I feel fine." The dizziness had gone, or never come. She looked steadily at Gabriel. In the moonlight his eyes were as black as his hair, and his

74

pale face was almost supernaturally beautiful. "I'm psychic, so I have more of the energy than normal people. Obviously I've got enough to spare."

"It was still a risk. And if you touch me, there's the risk I'll take more."

"But you're all right now. You said so, and I can feel it, too. You don't need more; you're all right."

There was a pause and Gabriel's eyes dropped. Then, slowly, almost grudgingly, he said, "Yes." Kaitlyn could feel him trying to think, could sense his confusion. "And—I'm grateful," he said at last. He said it awkwardly, as if he hadn't had much practice, but when he lifted his eyes again she saw that he meant it. She could feel it, too, a childlike, marveling gratitude that was totally at odds with those chiseled features and grim mouth.

Kait's throat tightened. It was all she could do not to reach out to him again. Instead she said, as dispassionately as she could manage, "Gabriel, was it the crystal?"

"What?" He looked away from her again, as if realizing he'd revealed too much.

"You weren't like this before. You didn't *need* energy, not before Mr. Zetes hooked you up with that crystal. But now you've got a mark on your forehead, and you've changed—"

"Into a real psychic vampire." Gabriel laughed shortly. "That's what the people at the research center in Durham said—but they didn't know, did they? Nobody can know what the reality is like."

"That isn't what I was going to say. I was going to say that you'd changed, and I'd noticed it before

75

tonight. I think you've become—more powerful. You can link up with minds outside the web, and before you couldn't."

Gabriel was rubbing his forehead absently but roughly. "I suppose it had to be the crystal," he said. "Who knows, maybe that's what it's for. Maybe it's what Zetes wanted, all of us slaves to this—need."

The idea took Kaitlyn's breath away. She'd been thinking of it as some side effect, something that had happened accidentally because the crystal had burned too much of Gabriel's energy. But the idea that anyone would do this deliberately—would make someone like this on *purpose* . . .

"It's nauseating, isn't it?" Gabriel said conversationally. "What I've become is nauseating. And I'm afraid it's permanent, or at least I don't see any reason why it shouldn't be."

He'd seen her horror and was hurt by it. Kait tried to think of some way to make him feel better, and settled on brisk normalcy.

"Well, at least we have a way of dealing with it," she said. "For now, we'd better get this girl back to where she came from, don't you think? And then we should go and tell Rob. He'll want to help and he may even be able to think—"

She broke off with a gasp. She'd been getting to her feet, but now Gabriel hauled her back down again with one powerful yank.

Kaitlyn found herself looking into eyes that were black and glittering with menacing fury.

7

"No," Gabriel snarled. "We will not tell Rob—*anything.*"

Kaitlyn was bewildered. "But—the others have to know—"

"They don't have to know. They're not my *keepers.*"

"Gabriel, they'll *want* to know. They care about you, too. And Rob may be able to help you."

"I don't want his help."

It was said flatly, and with absolute finality. Kaitlyn realized that on this issue Gabriel was inflexible, and there was no use in arguing.

He went on anyway, just in case she needed convincing. "Of course, I can't stop *you* from telling them," he said, releasing her arm and giving a sudden disarming smile. "But if you do I'm afraid I'll have to leave this little expedition . . . and our group . . . permanently."

Kaitlyn rubbed her arm. "All right, Gabriel. I get

the point. And," she added with sudden conviction, "I'll still help you. But you've got to *let* me help. You've got to tell me when you're feeling—like you did tonight. You've got to come to me, instead of wandering around looking for girls to attack."

Gabriel's expression was suddenly bleak. "Maybe I don't want your help, either," he said stonily. Then he burst out, "How long do you think you can keep this up? This *donation?* Even a psychic doesn't have endless energy. What if you get weak?"

That's why I wanted to tell Rob, Kaitlyn thought, but she knew better than to start debating again. She simply said, "We'll deal with that when we come to it." She tried to hide the flicker of unease inside her. What *would* they do—if Gabriel had one of these fits and she was too weak to help him? He'd kill an ordinary person, drain him dry.

Think about it later, she decided. And then pulled out the old hope, the one that had been comforting her since they'd left the Institute.

"Maybe the people in the white house can help," she said. "Maybe they'll know a way to cure you— undo what the crystal did."

"If it was the crystal," Gabriel said. With a faint self-mocking smile he added, "It seems to me that we're expecting a lot from these people in the white house."

That's because we don't have any other hope. Kaitlyn didn't say it, but she knew Gabriel understood. She and Gabriel sometimes understood each other too well.

"Let's get this girl back. What car did she come

from?" she asked, turning away from those ironic dark
gray eyes.

They put the girl back in the Cadillac. According to
Gabriel, she'd been alone, which was fortunate. Nobody would have noticed she was missing, or called
the police. And Gabriel said that she'd never seen
him—he'd come up behind her and put her to sleep
with one touch of his mind.

"I seem to be developing new talents by the hour,"
he said and smiled.

Kaitlyn wasn't amused, but she had to admit to
some relief. The girl would just think she'd fallen
asleep and would drive away never knowing what had
happened to her. Or at least that was what Kait hoped.

"You'd better get in the van with the rest of us," she
said. "You need *sleep.*"

Gabriel didn't object. A few minutes later he was
settling down in the other bucket seat, while Kait was
creeping into the back of the van again.

I need sleep, too, she thought, snuggling in beside
Rob's warm body with a feeling of gratitude. And,
please, please, I don't want any more dreams.

When Kaitlyn woke again, it was daylight. Rob was
sitting up, and all around her were the noises of people
stirring and yawning.

"How is everybody?" Rob asked. His blond hair
was tousled and he looked terribly young, Kaitlyn
thought. Young and vulnerable when you compared
his sleepy golden eyes to the dark gray ones she'd seen
last night. . . .

"Kinked up," Lewis moaned from the front. He was

wriggling his shoulders. Kaitlyn had a few kinks herself, and she saw that Gabriel was stretching cautiously.

"You'll be fine," Anna said and got up. She opened the side door and jumped lightly out, with no sign of stiffness.

"I feel like I swallowed a fuzz ball," Rob said, running his tongue over his teeth. "Does anybody—"

Oh, my God. What is *it?*

The exclamation came from outside the van, from Anna. The four inside immediately broke off what they were doing and started for the door.

What's wrong, Anna? Kaitlyn thought even before she got out.

I've never seen anything like it.

Anna's grave dark eyes were wide, fixed on the van itself. Kaitlyn turned and looked, but at first couldn't quite grasp what she was seeing. It looked almost *beautiful* at first.

The entire van was swathed with glittering ribbons —as if someone had painted stripes of shining stuff all over it, even over the windows. In the crisp morning light the stripes took on rainbow colors. There were hundreds of the bands, crossing and recrossing.

And yet it wasn't beautiful, really. It evoked a feeling of revulsion in Kait. When she looked closely at one of the stripes, she saw it was tacky . . . slimy, almost. Like . . . like *mucus* . . .

"Slug trails!" Rob said and pulled Kaitlyn away from the van.

Kaitlyn's stomach lurched. She was glad she hadn't eaten more for dinner last night.

"Slug trails—but it *can't* be," Gabriel said, sounding angry. "Look around you—there's no sign of a trail anywhere but on the van."

It was true. Kaitlyn swallowed and said, "I've never seen a slug big enough to leave a trail like *that.*"

"I have, in *Planet of the Giant Gastropods,*" Lewis said.

"I have, too, in my backyard," Anna said. She nodded when the others looked at her. "I'm serious. In Puget Sound there are slugs that big, banana slugs. Some people eat them."

"Thank you for sharing that with us," Kaitlyn whispered, stomach lurching again.

Gabriel still looked angry. "How did they get there?" he demanded, as if Anna had put them there personally. "And why aren't there any on those cars?" He pointed toward a gray Buick parked nearby, and the middle-aged couple in the Buick looked at him curiously.

"Leave her alone. She doesn't know," Rob said before Anna could answer.

"Do *you?*"

Rob slanted a dangerous golden glare at Gabriel and started to shake his head. Then he stopped and looked thoughtful. He turned to the van again, frowning.

"It could be—"

"What?" Kaitlyn asked.

Rob shook his head slowly. In the early sunlight he looked like a ruffled golden angel. "Oh, nothing," he said and shrugged.

Kait had the feeling that he was suppressing something, and the next minute he gave her a half-laughing look, as if to say she wasn't the only one who could hide things in the web.

A nasty *stubborn* angel, Kait thought, and Rob grinned.

"Come on, let's get out of this place," he said, turning to the others, who were looking displeased. "It's just slug stuff. Let's find a car wash."

Until that moment Kaitlyn had forgotten her dream about the colorless people. The episode with Gabriel had swamped it, somehow, driving it back into her subconscious. But now, suddenly, she remembered, and she looked at the van sharply.

"Heads up!" Lewis hissed before she could say anything. "It's the law!"

A police car was cruising into the rest stop. Kaitlyn's heart gave one thump, and then she was following the others in a quick but orderly retreat into the van.

Just keep your heads down and stay calm, Rob told them. *Pretend you're talking to each other.*

"A lot of good that's going to do," Gabriel said acidly.

The police car drove past them. Kait couldn't help glancing sideways at it. A uniformed woman in the passenger seat glanced up at the same moment, and for an instant their eyes met.

Kaitlyn's breath stopped. She only hoped her face was as utterly blank as her mind felt. If that police-woman saw her terror . . .

The car cruised on.

Kait's could feel her pulse in her throat. *Somebody start driving,* she thought. *Fast but casual.* Rob was already sliding into the driver's seat.

Kaitlyn was still terrified the police car would turn around, or follow them when they left. But it didn't. It seemed to have stopped at the other end of the rest stop.

Where the white Cadillac was, Kait's mind supplied, and she tried to squash the thought and the memories it evoked instantly. She didn't dare look at Gabriel or let herself wonder if the curly haired girl *had* remembered something after all.

"Don't be scared," Lewis said when they were once again on Highway 5. He'd felt her turmoil even if he didn't know the reason. "We're okay now."

Kaitlyn gave him a watery smile.

They found a do-it-yourself car wash in a town called Grants Pass, and Kaitlyn disbursed ninety-nine cents from their funds to buy paper towels. She also paid for breakfast burritos and coffee at a McDonald's, since none of them could face peanut butter this early in the morning.

"And now we should cut over to the coast," Rob said when they were done eating. They'd washed themselves as well as the car at the car wash, a novel experience that Kait wasn't sure she wanted to repeat.

"Well, you have two choices," said Lewis, who had by default become the Keeper of the Map. "There's a road that goes through the Siskiyou National Forest, and then a little north of that there's a regular highway."

After a short discussion they decided on the highway. As Anna said, the white house might be surrounded by trees, but it wasn't in a landlocked forest. It was someplace where the ocean came between two wooded arms of land.

"Some place called Griffin's Pit," Lewis said, his eyes crinkling as he looked at Kait.

"We might try looking that up in a library some-where," Rob said, steering the van back to the free-way. "That and all the other variations we can think of."

"Maybe we'll just *find* the place first," Kaitlyn said wistfully.

But at Coos Bay, where the highway finally reached the coast, she slumped and shook her head.

"Not north enough," she said and glanced at Anna for confirmation.

Anna was nodding resignedly. They all stood around the van, staring down at the ocean. It was vast and blue and sparkling—and *wrong*. Not at all like the water they'd seen in the dream.

"It's way too civilized," Anna said. She pointed to a large freighter loaded with logs that was passing through the bay entrance. "See that? It's putting junk in the water—oil or gasoline or something—and the water we saw wasn't *like* that. It wasn't traveled like this. It felt clean."

"Felt clean," Gabriel repeated, almost sneering.

"Yes," Kaitlyn said. "It did. And look at those sand dunes. Did anybody see sand in the dream?"

"No." Rob sighed. "Okay, back in the van. Yukon ho."

"Can't we eat first?" Lewis pleaded. It had taken them until noon to get to the bay.

"Eat while we drive," Rob said. In the van Kaitlyn made and passed out peanut butter sandwiches.

They chewed on them apathetically, looking out the windows. The view as they drove north up the Oregon coast was not inspiring.

"Sand," Lewis said after half an hour. "I never knew there was so much sand in the world."

The dunes seemed endless. They were huge and rolling, sometimes blocking off the view of the ocean. In places they were hundreds of feet high.

"How horrible," Kaitlyn said suddenly. In the sand she could see distant trees—buried trees. Only the top third of their trunks emerged from the dune, standing but quite dead. It was as if the dunes had swallowed a forest . . . and digested it.

"Jeez, there's even vultures circling," Lewis said, eyeing a large bird.

"That's an osprey," Anna said almost unkindly.

Kait glanced at her, then sat back, relapsing into silence. She felt depressed, and she didn't know if it was the dunes, the prospect of endless traveling to an unknown destination, or the peanut butter sandwiches.

Everyone else was silent, too. There was a heavy feeling to the air. Oppressive. Laced with something Kaitlyn couldn't quite put her finger on. . . .

"Oh, come on," she said, half aloud. "Cheer up, everybody. This is only our second day." She groped in her mind for an interesting topic to distract them. After a moment she found one, not only interesting but slightly dangerous. Oh, well, nothing ventured, nothing gained.

"So, Lewis, about this *chi* stuff," she said. He glanced at her lethargically. "So, I was wondering, how much can somebody afford to lose before they get sick?"

She could see Gabriel stiffen in the front passenger seat.

"Um," Lewis said. "It depends. Some people have a lot—they generate it all the time. If you're healthy you do that, and it just kind of flows freely inside you, without any blocks. Through strange channels."

Kaitlyn laughed. "Through what?"

"Strange channels. Really. That's what my grandfather called some of the arteries the *chi* runs through. He was a master of *chi gong*—that's the art of manipulating *chi,* kind of like what Rob does when he heals."

Gabriel by now was deliberately *not* looking at Kait, all the while willing her fiercely to shut up. Unable to send a reassuring message, Kaitlyn ignored him.

"So it's sort of like blood," she said to Lewis. "And if you lose it, you manufacture more."

"In the Middle Ages people thought blood *was* the life energy," Rob said from the driver's seat. "They thought some people had too much—that's what they had in mind when they bled you with leeches. They thought if they could drain some of the extra blood off, it would relieve the pressure; help you produce better, clearer blood afterward. But of course they were wrong—about blood."

He looked over his shoulder as he said it, and Kait thought his glance encompassed Gabriel as well as her. Alarm shot through her. Rob wasn't stupid. What if he'd guessed . . . ?

Gabriel was radiating cold fury.

"Well, that's interesting," Kait gabbled. She now wanted to find a boring topic to make them all forget this. Even silence would be fine—but Rob was speaking again.

"Some people think that's how the legends of

vampires started," he said. "With psychics that drained their victims of life energy, *sekhem, chi,* whatever you want to call it. Later the stories got twisted and people called it blood."

Kaitlyn sat frozen. It wasn't just what Rob was saying, it was the *way* he was saying it. His disgust and loathing filled the web.

"I've heard legends about that, too," Anna said, and her repugnance was equally clear. "About evil shamans who live by stealing power from others."

"That's sick," said Lewis. "If a *chi gong* master did that, he'd be ostracized. It completely violates the Tao."

Their abhorrence was reverberating in the web, shuddering over Kaitlyn in waves. Very distantly she could sense Gabriel's stony presence.

No wonder he didn't want them to know, she thought, knowing that no one else could sense her through the all-pervading horror and aversion. None of them can understand. They just think it's awful.

She wished she could tell Gabriel she was sorry, but Gabriel was looking out the window, his shoulders tense.

To Kaitlyn's vast relief, Lewis changed the subject. "And of course there are the people whose energy fields are too *strong,"* he said with a sly look at Rob. "You know, the people you agree with even when you don't know why. The ones that put you under a spell with their charisma—their energy just knocks you out."

Rob's eyes in the rearview mirror were innocent. "If I see somebody like that I'll tell you," he said. "Sounds dangerous."

"It is. You can find yourself fighting evil magicians just because some nut thought it was a good idea."

There was an edge to Lewis's voice that showed the remark wasn't entirely benign. Kaitlyn was glad they weren't talking about vampires anymore, but discouraged when everyone lapsed into silence again.

Something's wrong with us, she thought, and shivered.

The silence lasted for endless miles up the coast. The dunes ran out eventually and were replaced by black basalt headlands that plunged down to the sea. Huge waves crashed around strange rocks rising like monoliths out of the water.

At one point they passed a deep fissure in the cliffs, where the pounding sea had whipped the water into a froth like cream.

"Devil's Churn," Lewis said sepulchrally, raising his head from the map.

"Looks like it," Kaitlyn said. She meant to sound lighthearted, but somehow it came out grim.

Silence again. They passed offshore islands, but these were inhabited only by gulls and other birds. No trees, no white house. Kaitlyn shivered again.

"We're never going to find it," Lewis said.

This was so unlike him that Kait felt only surprise, but Anna turned sharply. "I wish you wouldn't be so pessimistic. Or if you have to be, I wish you'd keep your opinions to yourself!"

Kaitlyn's jaw dropped. The next moment she felt a rush of protective anger. "You don't have to be so nasty to him," she told Anna heatedly. "Just because you're so—so *stoic* all the time. . . ." She stopped and almost bit her tongue. What had made her say that?

Hurt flashed in Anna's dark eyes. Lewis scowled. "I can fight my own battles," he said. "You're always jumping in."

"Yes, she's a real little do-gooder," Gabriel said from the front.

Rage exploded in Kaitlyn. "And you're a cold-blooded *snake!*" she shouted. Gabriel gave her a brilliant, unsettling smile.

"She got that one right, anyway," Rob said. The van was swerving erratically. Rob was looking at Gabriel rather than at the road. "And you shut up, Lewis, if you know what's good for you."

"I think you're all horrible," Anna gasped. She seemed on the verge of tears. "And I've *had* it, all right? You can let me off here because I'm not going with you any farther."

Tires squealed as Rob hit the brakes. A horn blared behind them.

"Fine," Rob said. "Get out."

8

"Go on," Rob said curtly. "Don't keep us all waiting."

The horn blared again behind them.

Anna rose without any of her usual grace. Her movements were jerky, full of repressed energy. She snatched up her duffel bag and began to fumble with the door handle.

Kait sat stiffly, her shoulders tense, her head high. Her heart was pounding with defensive fury. *Let* Anna go if she wanted. It just showed she'd never cared for the rest of them in the first place.

Ridiculous.

The thought came out of nowhere, like a tiny glint of light in her mind, there and gone in an instant. It was enough to shock Kaitlyn into some kind of sense.

Ridiculous—of course Anna cared for the rest of them. Anna cared about everything, from the earth itself to the animals she loved to just about any person that crossed her path.

But then why was Kait so *angry* with her? Kait could feel all the physical symptoms. The pounding heart, the shortness of breath—the flushed face and tight feeling at her temples. More, there was a wild need to *move* in her muscles, like the desire to hit something.

Physical symptoms. It was another glint, surfacing from Kaitlyn's subconscious. And suddenly she understood.

"Anna, wait. *Wait,*" she said just as Anna wrestled the door open. She tried to make her voice calm, when it kept wanting to come out panicked or seething.

Anna stopped but didn't turn.

"Don't you see—everybody, don't you *see?*" Kaitlyn looked around at the others. "This isn't real. We're all upset, but we're not really upset at each other. We're just *feeling* angry, so our minds think there must be a reason to *be* angry."

"It's just nerves, I suppose," Gabriel sneered. His lip was curled and his gray eyes were savage. "We couldn't possibly really hate each other."

"No! I don't know what it is, but—" Kaitlyn broke off, realizing that in addition to all the other physical symptoms she was shivering. It was *cold* in the van, colder than could be explained by the open door. And there was a strange odor in her nostrils, a sewer stench.

"Do you smell that? It's the same thing I smelled yesterday when Lewis did his sleepwalking bit. And it's cold like yesterday, too." Kaitlyn could see confusion mingling with the anger in the faces around her, and she turned to the one person she trusted absolutely.

Rob, she said fervently, *please listen. I know it's hard because you* feel *like you're angry, but just try. Something's going on.*

Slowly Rob's face cleared. The smoldering fury went out of his amber-colored eyes, leaving them golden and somewhat bewildered. He blinked and put a hand to his forehead.

"You're right," he said. "It's like that psychology experiment—give someone an injection of adrenaline, and then put them in a room with someone acting angry. The first person gets angry, too, but it's not real anger. It's been *induced.*"

"Someone's doing that to us," Kaitlyn said.

"But how?" Lewis demanded. He sounded scoffing, but not as exasperated as before. "Nobody's given us any injections."

"Long distance," Rob said. "It's a psychic attack."

His voice was flat and positive. His eyes had gone dark gold. Outside, the blaring horn had given way to several horns sounding continuously.

"Shut the door, Anna," Rob said quietly. "I'll find a place to pull over. There's something I ought to have told you before."

Anna slid the door shut. A few minutes later they had pulled over by the roadside and Rob was looking at the rest of them soberly.

"I should have mentioned it this morning," he said. "But I wasn't sure, and I didn't see any point in you all worrying. Those slug tracks . . . well, back at Durham I heard stories about people waking up to find those around their house. Slime trails or sometimes footprints of people or animals. They almost always went along with nightmares—people having terrible dreams the night before."

Nightmares. Now Kaitlyn remembered. "I had a terrible dream last night," she said. "There were all these people leaning over me. Gray people—they looked like pencil sketches. And it was cold—just the way it was a few minutes ago." She looked at Rob. "But what *is* it?"

"They said all those things were signs of a psychic attack."

"A psychic attack," Gabriel repeated, but his tone was less sarcastic than it had been.

"The stories were that dark psychics could do things even over long distances. They could visualize you and use PK, telepathy, even astral projection." His troubled eyes turned back to Kait. "Those gray people you saw—I've heard that astral projections are colorless."

"Astral projections as in letting your mind do the walking? Leaving your body behind?" Lewis asked, cocking an eyebrow. The atmosphere had changed; the web was no longer quivering with animosity. Kait thought that everyone looked like themselves again.

Rob was nodding. "That's it. And I've heard that psychic attacks can make you weak or nervous—even make you think you're going crazy."

"I thought *I* was going crazy just now," Anna said. Her eyes were large and bright with unshed tears. "I'm sorry, everybody."

"I'm sorry, too," Kaitlyn said. She and Anna looked at each other a moment and then simultaneously reached forward to hug each other.

"Sure, everybody's sorry," Gabriel said impatiently. "But we've got more important things to think about. A psychic attack means one thing—we've been found."

"Mr. Zetes," Rob said.

"Who else? But the question is, who's he gotten to do it? What psychics are attacking?"

Kaitlyn tried to visualize the faces in her dream. It was impossible. The features had been too blurred.

"Mr. Z had a lot of contacts," Rob said wearily. "Obviously he's found some new friends."

Anna was shaking her head. "But how can he have found such powerful ones so fast? I mean, *we* couldn't do what they're doing, and we're supposed to be the best."

"The best of our age group," Rob began, but Kaitlyn said, "The crystal."

Understanding flared immediately in Gabriel's eyes. "That's it. The crystal is amplifying their power."

"But it's *dangerous,*" Kaitlyn started, and then she shut up at an ominous glance from Gabriel.

Intent on his own thoughts, Rob didn't seem to notice. "Obviously, they don't care about the danger, and while they're using the crystal they're much stronger than we are. The point is that we've got to be prepared. They're not finished with us—and the attacks will probably get worse. We've got to be ready for anything."

"Yeah, but ready how?" asked Lewis. "What can you do against that kind of attack?"

Rob shrugged. "At the Durham Center I heard people talk about envisioning light—protective light.

The problem is that I never really listened. I don't know how you do it."

Kaitlyn let out her breath and sat back. The others were doing the same, and a sense of apprehension ran through the web. Apprehension—and vulnerability.

There was a long silence.

"Well, I suppose we'd better get back on the road," Kait said finally. "It's no good sitting around and thinking about it."

"Just everybody be on the lookout for anything unusual," Rob said.

But nothing unusual happened on the rest of the drive. Anna took the wheel and they resumed their beach-scanning, agreeing that nothing on the Oregon coast looked like the place in their dreams. The rock was too black—volcanic, apparently—and the water too open.

"And it's still not north enough," Kait said.

They stopped that night at a little town called Cannon Beach, just below the Washington border. It was already dark by the time Anna pulled the van into a quiet street that dead-ended on the beach.

"This may not be legal, but I don't think anybody's going to bother us," she said. "For that matter, I've hardly seen anybody around here."

"It's a resort town," Rob said. "And this is off season."

It certainly seemed like off season to Kaitlyn. The sky was clouding over, and it was cold and windy outside.

"I saw a little store back there on the main street," she said. "We've got to buy something for dinner—we ate the last of the bread and peanut butter for lunch."

DARK VISIONS

"I'll go," Anna said. "I don't mind the cold."

Rob nodded. "I'll go with you."

It was only once they were gone that Kait wished Lewis had gone, too. She was getting worried about Gabriel.

He seemed tense and distant, staring out the window into the dark. In the web Kaitlyn could feel only coldness and a sense of walls—as if he were living in a castle of ice.

He put the highest walls up when he had the most to hide, Kaitlyn knew. Right now she was worried that he was suffering—and that he wouldn't come to her for help.

And she'd noticed something else. He was still sitting in the front passenger seat. The rest of them had changed places every so often, but Gabriel always stuck to the front.

I wonder, Kait thought, if it could have anything to do with the fact that *I* always stick to the back.

She was getting fairly good at screening her thoughts when she concentrated. Neither Lewis nor Gabriel seemed to have heard that.

Rob and Anna returned windblown and laughing, clutching paper bags to their chests.

"We splurged," Rob said. "Microwave hot dogs—they're still pretty hot—and Nachos and potato chips."

"And Oreos," Anna said, puffing back wisps of black hair that had blown in her face.

Lewis grinned as he unwrapped a hot dog. "Pure junk food. Joyce would die."

Kaitlyn glanced at him, and for a moment everyone stilled. We still can't really believe it, Kait thought. We all *know* Joyce betrayed us, but we can't accept it. How could anyone put on an act the way she did?

"She was so—*alive*," Anna said. "Effervescent. Energetic. I liked her from the minute I saw her."

"And she used that," Gabriel snarled. "She was recruiting us; making us like her was just a technique."

So tense, Kaitlyn thought. He's incredibly on edge. She watched Gabriel tearing into a hot dog almost savagely, and worry shifted in her stomach.

"Really hits the spot, doesn't it?" she said. Her eyes were on Gabriel, and she tried to keep her presence in the web completely neutral. She added casually, "But maybe it's not enough."

"We got two for everybody and a couple of extras," Anna said, following Kait's gaze to Gabriel. "You can have one of the extras, Gabriel."

He waved her off impatiently. His gray eyes, fixed on Kaitlyn, were full of angry warning.

"Just trying to be helpful," Kaitlyn said. She leaned close to Gabriel to fish a potato chip out of the bag and added in a low voice, "I wish you'd let me."

You can help by leaving me alone.

The thought was swift and brutal—and meant only for her. Kaitlyn could tell that none of the others had heard it. Trust Gabriel to have perfected the art of private communication.

So he wasn't going to come to her. He needed to, she was sure of that now. His face seemed even paler than usual, almost chalky, and there was a repressed violence to his movements. As if he were under some terrible internal pressure, and in danger of flying apart at any minute.

But he was stubborn, and that meant he wouldn't come. Gabriel didn't know how to ask for help, he only knew how to take.

Never mind, Kaitlyn thought, watching him surreptitiously. I'm stubborn, too. And I'm *damned* if I'm going to let you kill yourself—or anybody else.

Gabriel waited until they were all asleep.

Kaitlyn had been the last to succumb, fighting even the warmth they'd produced by running the van's heaters before they bedded down. He'd felt the red-gold shimmer of her thoughts running on when all the others were still and silent. She was trying to outwait him.

But it didn't work. Gabriel could be patient when he had to be.

When even Kaitlyn's thoughts had faded into a humming blank, Gabriel quietly sat up in the driver's seat and opened the door beside him. He slid out and had the door shut again almost before anyone could stir. Then he waited a moment, his senses focused on the inside of the van.

Still asleep. Good.

The wind out here was bitterly cold. Not the sort of night for any sensible person to be out wandering. That was a problem, and Gabriel thought about it as he trudged through the dry, loose sand above the high tide line.

Then he looked up. There were cottages and duplexes on the beach, as well as motel units. And some of them must be occupied.

He tried to dredge up a killing smile, but he couldn't

quite manage. Breaking and entering was one crime he'd never committed before. Somehow it seemed different from picking a victim at random off the streets.

But the other choice was Kaitlyn.

This time the killing smile came easily. It was a smile for himself, and full of self-mockery. Because Kaitlyn was the obvious choice—the girl was warm and willing and definitely pleasant to link up with. Her life energy encased her in a scintillating ruby glow; her mind was a place of blue pools and blazing meteors. He'd been tempted all day by the aura that surrounded her like a charged field.

It had been all he could do not to plunge into that halo and drink it in gulps. Find a transfer point and fix on to it like a leech. He'd needed her desperately.

Only a complete fool would have turned down her help when it was freely offered.

Fighting his way through crumbling sand while the wind lashed around him like a lost spirit, Gabriel smiled.

Then he began to trudge toward one of the cottages that had a light in the window.

Kait woke up and cursed herself.

She'd been absolutely determined not to fall asleep. And now Gabriel was gone, of course. She could feel his absence.

How could she have been so *stupid*?

She'd had practice, now, in disentangling herself from Rob and slipping away soundlessly.

Kait almost yelped as she stepped away from the

van and into the wind. She should have brought a jacket—but it was no use thinking about that now. Head bent, arms wrapped around herself, she cast her thoughts wide.

She'd had practice now in searching for Gabriel, too. He was good at concealing himself, but she knew what to look for. In only a moment she had found it—a faraway sense of glittering ice. Like a blue-white spark on the edge of her mind. Kait turned her body toward it and started walking.

It was rough going. The wind blew sheets of sand away from her. When the moon came out, it showed particles whisking through the air like ghosts. It also showed a gigantic rock shaped like a haystack rearing out of the ocean, where no rock had any business being.

A spooky place. Kaitlyn tried not to think about psychic attacks and Mr. Zetes. She was crazy to have come out here alone, of course—but what else could she do?

The wind smelled of saltwater. From her left came the soft-but-loud crashing of waves. Kait swerved to avoid driftwood and then turned sharply, heading for a cluster of cottages. There. Gabriel was very close; she could feel it.

The next moment she saw him; a dark silhouette against a lighted window. Alarm spurted through her. That window—she knew what he was doing loitering around a cottage. What if he'd already . . .

Gabriel!

The call was involuntary, wrung out of her by panic. Kaitlyn's heart thumped before she realized that Rob and the others were out of range.

Gabriel wasn't. His head whipped around.

What are you doing here?

What are you *doing?* she countered. *What have you done, Gabriel?*

She saw him hesitate, then saw him abandon the cottage window abruptly and come striding toward her. She walked to meet him, and he pulled her into the shelter of a carport.

"Can't I take a walk without being followed?" he said venomously.

Kaitlyn gave herself a moment before answering. She was trying to smooth her hair, which the wind had turned into a mane of elf-locks and fine tangles. And she needed to catch her breath.

At last she looked at him. A streetlight outside illuminated half his face, leaving the other half in shadow. Kaitlyn could see enough. His skin looked tight, as if it had been stretched over his bones. There were black circles under his eyes. And there was something about his expression . . . the way he stared at her, eyes narrowed, lips drawn back a little as he breathed quickly.

Gabriel was on the breaking point. And, no, he hadn't gotten into that cottage yet.

"Is that what you were doing?" she said. "Taking a walk?"

"Yes." His lips drew back a little farther. His eyes had turned defiant—he was going to brazen this out. "I need to get away from the rest of you once in a while. There's only so much of Kessler's mind I can stand."

"So you just wanted some privacy." She took a step

toward him. "And you decided now was the time for a little stroll."

With startling suddenness he flashed his most dazzling smile. "Exactly."

Kait took another step. The smile disappeared as suddenly as it had come, leaving his mouth grim. "In the middle of the night. In the freezing cold."

He looked dangerous now. Dark and dangerous as a wolf on the hunt. "That's right, Kait. Now be a good girl and go back to the van."

Kaitlyn moved again, close enough that she could feel his warmth—and he could feel hers. She could feel the instant tension in his body, could see his eyes darken. She could hear his breath become uneven.

"I've never been a good girl. Ask anybody back home—they said I have an attitude problem. So you were just hanging around that cottage by accident."

He took the sudden change in subject without blinking, but when he spoke it was through clenched teeth. "What else would I be doing?"

"I thought"—Kaitlyn tilted her head back to look up at him—"that you might need something."

"I don't need anything from anyone!"

She'd accomplished something astonishing just then—she'd made Gabriel give way before her. He'd retreated, stepping back until the concrete wall behind him stopped him.

Kait didn't give him a chance to regroup. She knew the risk of what she was doing. Gabriel was on the verge of snapping—and he was capable of violence. But she wouldn't let herself think about the danger; she could only think about the shining torment in Gabriel's eyes.

She moved to him again, this time so close that they were touching. Carefully, deliberately, she put her hands on his chest. She could feel the running-stag clamor of his heart.

Then she looked up at him, her face inches from his. "I think you're lying," she whispered.

9

Something in Gabriel's eyes fractured. It was like watching gray agate shatter into pieces.

He caught Kaitlyn by the shoulder. His other hand clamped in her hair, twisting her head to the side.

Black terror washed over Kait, but she didn't move. Her fingers tightened on the sleeves of Gabriel's borrowed shirt.

Then she felt his lips on the back of her neck.

The first sensation was a piercing, as if a single sharp tooth had penetrated at the upper part of her spine, just below her neck.

Vampires, Kait thought dazedly. She knew Gabriel was just opening a transfer point, but it felt as if he had punctured her skin. She could easily see how the legends about vampires had started.

The next instant the sharp pain had gone, replaced by a *tugging*, as if something inside her was being plucked up by the roots. She felt her own momentary resistance—like the Earth clinging to a handful of weeds being pulled. And then a giving, a yielding. As if the weeds had come free in the pulling hand.

Energy fountained out of the open wound in a narrow stream. Kaitlyn felt a flare of heat—and pleasure.

All right. It's going to be all right, she thought, scarcely knowing whether she was speaking to herself or Gabriel. The experience itself was frightening—it was like working with high-voltage electricity. But she refused to be afraid on other grounds.

I trust you, Gabriel, she thought.

She could feel the energy pouring into him, and once again she felt his gratitude, his appreciation. His relief as his need was met.

I trust you.

The energy was still flowing steadily, and Kait had a sense of cleansing. Her entire body felt light and airy, as if her feet weren't touching the ground. She relaxed in Gabriel's arms, letting him support her.

Thank you.

The thought wasn't Kaitlyn's, and no one else was in range—so it had to be Gabriel. But it didn't sound like Gabriel. There was no anger, no mockery. It was the free and joyous communication of a happy child.

Then, all at once, the current streaming between them was broken. Gabriel released her and lifted his head.

Dizzy, Kaitlyn clung to him for a moment, hearing her own breath slowing.

"No more," Gabriel said. He was breathless, too, but calm. The starving emptiness inside him filled—at least partly.

Then he said, "Kait . . ."

Kaitlyn made herself let go of him. She stepped back, keeping her eyes down.

"Are—are you sure it's enough? You'll be okay now?" She spoke because sharing thoughts was too intimate.

It had occurred to her—finally—that she was courting another kind of danger here. Being this close to Gabriel, *giving* to him, and feeling his joy and gratification—it had bound them together in a way even the web could not match. It had brought down Gabriel's walls . . . again.

And that was unfair, because on her part it was just caring. It's not like what I feel for Rob, she told herself. It isn't—love. . . .

She could sense Gabriel looking at her. Then she felt an indefinable change in him, a mental straightening of shoulders.

"We need to get back," he said. His voice was short and he ignored her question.

Kait looked up. "Gabriel—"

"Before we're missed." Gabriel turned away and started out into the night.

But he waited for her after a few steps, and he stayed close as they made their way across the beach. Kaitlyn said nothing as they walked. She couldn't think of anything that wouldn't make matters worse.

As soon as they got within sight of the van, she saw that something was wrong.

The van should have been dark inside, but each window was glowing. For one instant Kait thought the others had turned on the dome light, and then she thought of fire. But the glow was too bright for the dome light and too cool for fire. And it had a strange opaque quality about it—almost like a phosphorescent mist.

Fear, icy and visceral, gripped at Kaitlyn.

"What is it?" she whispered.

Gabriel pushed her back. "Stay here."

He ran to the van, and Kait followed, scrambling up behind him when he opened the door. Instantly the trip-hammer beating of her heart seemed to double.

She could see the mist clearly now. And she could see Lewis in the front passenger seat and Anna curled on the first bench seat. They were both asleep—but not peacefully.

Lewis's face was twisted into a grimace, and he was moving his arms and legs jerkily as if trying to escape from something. Anna's long black hair hid her face, but she was writhing, one hand a claw.

"Anna!" Kaitlyn grasped her shoulder and shook her. Anna made a moaning sound, but didn't wake up.

"Rob!" Kaitlyn turned to him. He was lying on his back, thrashing helplessly. His eyes were shut, his expression one of agony. Kaitlyn shook him, too, calling his name mentally. Nothing helped.

She looked over to see how Gabriel was doing with Lewis—and froze.

The gray people were here.

She could see them hanging in the air between her and Gabriel. Lewis's seat cut right through one of them.

"It's an attack!" Gabriel shouted.

Kait was reeling. She felt giddy and confused, almost as if she might faint. It was the web, she realized—she was picking up the sensations of the three dreamers.

Oh, God—she had to do something fast, before she and Gabriel collapsed, too.

"Visualize light!" she shouted to Gabriel. "Remember what Rob said? You defend against psychic attacks by envisioning light!"

Gabriel turned his gray eyes on her. "Fine—just tell me how. And what *kind* of light?"

"I don't know." Panic was rioting inside Kaitlyn. "Just think about light—picture it all around us. Make it—a golden light."

She wasn't quite sure why she'd picked gold. Maybe because the mist was a sort of silvery-green. Or maybe because she always thought of gold as Rob's color.

Pressing her hands to her eyes, Kaitlyn began to envision light. Pure golden light surrounding all of them in the van. As an artist, she found it easy to hold the picture in her mind.

Like this, she thought to Gabriel and sent him the image. The next moment he was helping her, his conviction adding to hers. She felt she could actually *see* the light now; if she opened her eyes it would be there.

It's working, Gabriel told her.

It was. Kait's giddiness was fading, and for the first time since entering the van she felt warmth. The mist had been as cold as the outdoors.

It slipped away now, like an oppressive blanket sliding off Kait. Still visualizing the golden light, she opened her eyes.

The sleepers had quieted. The last traces of the mist were vanishing, curling in on themselves and disappearing. The gray people were still hanging in air.

The next instant they had vanished, too, but not

before Kaitlyn got a strange impression. For just a moment she had looked into one of those gray faces— and recognized it. It seemed *familiar,* although she couldn't put her finger on why.

Then the thought was driven out of her mind as she realized that Rob was stirring. He groaned and blinked, dragging himself to a sitting position.

"What—? Kaitlyn—?"

"Psychic attack," Kaitlyn told him calmly and precisely. "When we got back the whole van was filled with mist and you wouldn't wake up. We got rid of it by visualizing light. Oh, Rob, I was so scared." Abruptly her knees folded and she sat down on the floor.

Anna was sitting up, too, and Lewis was moaning.

"Are you guys okay?" Kaitlyn asked shakily, from the floor.

Rob clenched one hand in his unruly blond hair. "I had the most terrible nightmare. . . ." Then he looked at Kait and said, " 'When we got back?' "

Kaitlyn's mind went blank, which was probably a good thing. She was too shaken to summon a lie. But behind her Gabriel said smoothly, "Kait had to go to the bathroom, and she didn't want to go alone. I escorted her."

It was a good story. Rob and Anna had found a public rest room down the beach. But Kaitlyn felt little triumph when Rob nodded, accepting it. "Very gallant of you," he said wryly.

"We also saved you," Gabriel added pointedly. "Who knows what that mist was going to do?"

"Yes." Rob's face sobered. He tugged at his hair a moment and then looked up at Gabriel. "Thank you," he said, and his voice was frank and full of genuine emotion.

Gabriel turned away.

There was an awkward moment, and then Anna spoke up.

"Look, why don't you two explain just exactly how you 'visualized light,'" she said. "That way we'll know what to do if they attack again."

"And then maybe we can go back to *sleep,*" Lewis added.

Kait explained without much help from Gabriel. By the time she finished she was yawning hugely and her eyes were watering.

They settled down to sleep prepared for the worst, but nothing else happened that night, and Kaitlyn had no dreams.

She woke in the morning to Rob's mental exclamation. She hurried out of the van to find him and Anna bent over, staring at the ground beside the van.

The asphalt was covered with a thin layer of sand blown from the beach. In that sand, all around the van, were delicate tracks and footprints.

"They're animal tracks," Anna said. "You see these? These are the tracks of a raccoon." She pointed to a footprint three inches long, with five long splayed toes, each ending in a claw. "And these are from a fox." She moved her finger to a series of delicate four-toed marks.

"And those oval ones are from an unshod horse, and the little ones are from a rat," Anna finished. Then she looked up at Kait.

Kaitlyn didn't even bother saying, "But *all* of those

animals couldn't have been here last night." She remembered very well what Rob had said yesterday— sometimes victims of a psychic attack found the footprints of people or animals.

"Great," she muttered. "I have the feeling we should get out of here."

Rob stood up, brushing sand from his hands. "I agree."

It wasn't quite so easy, though, since the van picked that morning to be obstreperous. Rob and Lewis fiddled with the engine but could find nothing wrong, and in the end it started.

"I'll drive for a while," Anna said. She'd been sitting in the driver's seat, starting the engine when Rob told her to. "Just tell me where to go."

"Stay on 101 and we'll head into Washington," Lewis instructed. "But maybe we'd better stop at a McDonald's for breakfast first."

Kaitlyn wasn't sorry to say goodbye to the black basaltic Oregon coast. Gabriel had been edgy and silent all morning and she was beginning to wonder if what she'd done on the beach last night had been a mistake. She knew she would have to catch him sometime and talk it out, and the idea sent humming bees and butterflies into her stomach.

Please let us find the white house soon, she thought. And then, with a twinge, realized that Gabriel had been right. She *was* expecting a lot of the people in the white house. And what if they couldn't solve all the problems she was bringing them?

Kait shook her head, then turned to look at the dismal, slate-gray day outside.

They passed stands of what Anna said were alder

trees, which from a distance looked like big pink clouds. The alder branches were mostly bare, but there were a few reddish leaves hanging on each twig, which gave the stand an overall reddish cast.

By the side of the road were little kiosks which held huge bunches of daffodils, yellow as spring. Signs on the kiosks said $1.00 A BUNCH, but there was no one to take the money. It's the honor system, Kaitlyn thought. She longed for the pure gold of the daffodils, but she knew they couldn't spare the money.

Doesn't matter, she thought. I'll draw instead. She opened her kit and pulled out aureolin yellow, one of her favorite colors. In a few minutes she was drawing, glancing up only occasionally as they crossed a high bridge over the Columbia River. A sign proclaimed:

WELCOME TO WASHINGTON
THE EVERGREEN STATE

"You're home, Anna," Rob said.

"Not yet. It's a long way to Puget Sound if we're sticking to the coast," Anna replied, but Kaitlyn could tell from her voice that she was smiling.

"And we may not get there," Lewis put in. "We may find the white house first."

"Well, it's not here," Gabriel said shortly. "Look at the water."

The left side of the road, which dipped down to the ocean, was lined with large brown rocks and boulders. Nothing like the gray rocks in the dream.

Kaitlyn opened her mouth to say something—and her hand began to cramp.

A sort of itching cramp, a *need* that had her picking

up a pastel stick before she knew what she was doing. She knew what the sensations meant. Her gift was kicking in. Whatever she drew now would be not just a picture but a premonition.

Cool gray and burnt umber, steel and cloud blue. Kaitlyn watched her hand dotting and stroking the colors on, with no idea of what image was forming. All she knew was that it needed a touch of sepia here—and just two round circles of scarlet lake in the center.

When it was finished, she stared at it, feeling a strange creeping between her shoulderblades.

A goat. She'd drawn a *goat,* of all things. It was standing in what looked like a river of silvery-gray, surrounded by cloudy surrealistic fog. But that wasn't what frightened Kait. It was the eyes.

The goat's eyes were the only dash of color in the drawing. They were the color of burning coals, and they seemed to be looking straight out of the picture at Kaitlyn.

Rob's quiet voice made her jump. "What is it, Kait? And don't say 'nothing' this time—I know there's something wrong."

Mutely Kaitlyn held out the picture to him. He studied it, brows drawing together. His lips were a straight line.

"Do you have any idea what it means?" he asked.

Kaitlyn rubbed pastel dust between her fingers. "No. But then I never do—until it happens. All I know is that somewhere, somehow, I'm going to see that goat."

"Maybe it's symbolic," suggested Lewis, who was leaning over the back of the other bench seat to look.

Kaitlyn shrugged and said, "Maybe." She had a

nagging sense of guilt—what good was a gift that gave you this kind of premonition? She had produced the picture; she ought to be able to tell what it meant. Maybe if she concentrated . . .

She thought about it while they passed beaches of packed sand and mudflats—none of them like the white house terrain—and while they got lunch at a Red Apple Market. But all the concentration brought was a headache and a feeling of wanting to *do* something, something physical, to let off tension.

"I'll drive now," she said as they left the market.

Rob glanced at her. "Are you sure? You hate driving."

"Yes, but it's only fair," Kaitlyn said. "You've all taken a turn."

Driving the van wasn't as hard as she'd thought it would be. It was less responsive than Joyce's convertible, but the single-lane road was almost deserted and easy to follow.

After a while, though, it began to rain. It started with cat's-paw splatters that made a pleasant sound, but it got worse and worse. Soon it was raining violently—huge sheets that turned the windshield opaque in between sweeps of the wipers. As if someone were throwing buckets of silvery paint against the glass.

"Maybe someone else should drive now," Gabriel said from the bench seat behind Kaitlyn. He'd relinquished the front passenger seat when Kait had taken the wheel—as Kait had suspected he would.

She glanced at Rob, who'd taken the vacated seat. If it had been Rob's suggestion, she might have acquiesced. But Gabriel had a mocking, goading way of saying things that made you want to do just the opposite.

"I'm fine," she said shortly. "I think the rain is easing up."

"She's fine," Rob agreed, giving her one of his slow infectious smiles. "She can cope."

And then, of course, Kaitlyn was stuck with it. Tongue pressed against her front teeth, she peered into the rain and did her best to prove Rob right. The road straightened out and she drove faster, trying to demonstrate casual competence.

When it happened, it happened very suddenly. Later, Kaitlyn would wonder if it might have changed anything if Rob had been driving. But she didn't really think so. Nobody could have coped with what appeared on that narrow road.

Kait was almost convinced of her own competence when she saw the shape in the road. It was directly in her path but far enough ahead to avoid.

A gray shape. A low horned shape—a goat.

If Kaitlyn hadn't seen it before, she might not have recognized it—there was so little time. But she knew every line of that goat; she'd stared at it for hours this morning. It was exactly like her picture, down to the red eyes. They seemed to blaze at her, the only wink of color in the gray and rainy landscape.

Silver, some part of her mind thought wildly. The silvery-gray river hadn't been a river at all but a road. And the fog had been the rain-vapor rising from the ground.

But most of her mind wasn't thinking at all, it was just reacting. *Brakes,* it told her.

Kait's foot hit the brakes, pressing and releasing the

way her driver's ed teacher had advised for bad weather.

Nothing happened.

Her foot slammed down in utter defiance of the driver's ed teacher. And again, nothing happened. The van didn't skid; it didn't slow in the least.

The goat was dead ahead. There was no time to scream, no time even to think. No time to pay attention to the sudden clamor in the web as the others realized that something was wrong.

Kaitlyn wrenched at the steering wheel. The van swerved and careered to the left, into the opposite lane. She got a flash of trees getting close very fast.

Turn right! Swerve back!

Kait wasn't sure whose thought it was, but she was already obeying. The van swung right—too far.

I'm going off the road, she thought with a curious calm.

Then everything was confusion.

Kaitlyn could never really remember what happened next, except that it was awful. Trees whipped by. Branches hit the windshield. There was an impact —shocking—but it didn't seem to slow them.

Then the van seemed to leap and go rocketing downward.

Kaitlyn had a sense of being rattled around like a pea in a tin can. She could hear screaming—she thought it might be her own voice. And then there was another impact and everything went dark.

10

Kaitlyn could hear water—a musical gurgling sound. It was soothing and part of her wanted to listen to it and rest.

But she couldn't. There was something . . . someone she had to worry about. Someone . . .

Rob.

Not just Rob. The others. Something terrible had happened and she had to make sure they were all right.

Strangely, she wasn't sure just what had happened. All she knew was that it had been awful. She had to piece together just what the awful thing might have been from what she could see around her.

Opening her eyes, she found that she was in Marisol's van. The van wasn't moving and it wasn't on the road anymore. Through the windshield she could see trees, their branches dripping with green moss. Stretching in front of her she could see water. A creek.

For the first time, she realized that there was water around her feet.

Idiot! There was an accident!

As soon as she thought it, she looked over to Rob. He was blinking, trying to undo his seat belt, seeming as dazed as she felt.

Rob, are you okay? Instinctively Kait used the most intimate form of speech.

Rob nodded, still looking stupefied. There was a cut on his forehead. "Yeah—are you?"

"I'm sorry; I'm so sorry. . . ." If pressed, Kaitlyn couldn't have said what she was apologizing about. She only knew that she'd done something dreadful.

Forget sorry. We have to get out of here, Gabriel said.

Kaitlyn twisted to look behind her. "Are you guys all right? Is anybody hurt?"

"We're okay—I think," Lewis said. He and Anna were getting up. They didn't seem to be injured, but their faces were drained of color and their eyes stared wildly.

"Help me get this open," Gabriel said sharply, wrenching at the side door.

It took all three of them to get the door open, and then Kait and Rob had to crawl over the center console of the van to go out the same way. Jumping out of the van, Kaitlyn landed in water so cold it took her breath away. With Rob's help, she waded painfully over irregular stones to the bank.

From here she could see what had happened to the van. They'd gone off the road, hit a few trees, and then plunged down a steep embankment into the creek. Kaitlyn supposed it was lucky they'd finished right side up. The silver-blue van was dented and battered —the right front fender a mass of twisted metal.

"I'm sorry," she whispered. She now remembered what she had to be sorry for. She was doubly guilty— she'd lost control of the van and she'd failed to interpret her own drawing, the drawing that might have warned her.

"Don't worry, Kait," Rob said gently, putting his arms around her. But then he winced.

"Oh, Rob, your head—there's a terrible cut."

He put a hand to it. "Not that bad." But he squatted down on the fern-covered embankment. Rain dripped from the trees around him.

"We should wash it," Anna said. "We've got water, but we need some cloth—"

"My duffel bag!" Kaitlyn started into the water, but Gabriel held her back, seizing her arm ungently.

"That's dangerous, you idiot," he said. His gray eyes were hard.

"But I *need* it," Kaitlyn said. She felt that she could stop the shaking inside her if she just had something to *do,* some action to perform.

Gabriel's mouth twisted. "For God's sake—oh, all *right*. You stay here." Letting go of her so roughly it was almost a push, he turned and waded to the van. A moment later he was splashing back, holding not only Kait's bag, but Anna's, which contained the files Rob had taken from the hidden room.

"Thank you," Kaitlyn said, trying to look him in the eye.

"The blankets and sleeping bags are all soaked," Gabriel said briefly. "Not worth saving—we'll never dry them out in this weather."

Anna used a T-shirt of Kaitlyn's to wash Rob's cut and staunch the bleeding. Then she said, "Hold this, Kait," and went hiking up the embankment. She returned with a handful of something green.

"Hemlock needles," she said. "They're good for burns; maybe they'll help a cut, too." She applied them to Rob's head.

Lewis had been staring around at the dripping trees, twirling his baseball hat on one finger. Now he said abruptly, "Look, what happened? Did we skid or—"

"It was my fault," Kaitlyn said.

"No, it wasn't," Rob said stubbornly. The T-shirt bandage Anna had made hung over one eye, giving him the rakish look of a pirate. "There was a goat in the road."

Lewis stopped twirling his hat. "A goat."

"Yes. A gray goat . . ." Rob's voice trailed off and he looked at Kaitlyn. "Gray," he said. "Colorless, really."

Kaitlyn stared at him, then shut her eyes. "Oh."

Anna said, "You think it was an apparition? Like the gray people?"

"Of course it was," Kaitlyn said. She'd been so shaken by the accident that she'd forgotten what had happened just before. "I'm so stupid—it had red eyes. Like some sort of demon. And—oh, Rob!" She opened her eyes. "The brakes didn't work. I kept pressing and pressing, but they didn't work!" The trembling at her core seemed to expand suddenly until her whole body was shivering violently.

Rob put his arm around her, and she clung to him, trying to calm herself. "So it was a psychic attack," he said. "The goat was some kind of illusion—maybe an astral projection. At Durham I heard of psychics who could project a part of themselves in the shape of an animal. And the brakes had been tampered with—it must have been long-distance PK. The whole thing was a setup."

"And we could have been killed," Anna said thinly.

Gabriel's laugh was harsh. "Of course. They're playing for keeps."

Rob straightened his shoulders. "Well, the van's not worth salvaging—and besides, we'd better not let anybody find us here. They'll ask questions, want to call the police."

Kaitlyn could feel her heart skip a beat. She lifted her head to stare at Rob in dismay. "But—but, then, what do we *do?*"

"We go to my house," Anna said quietly. "My parents will help us."

Rob hesitated. "We agreed, no parents," he said. "We could end up putting them in danger—"

"But we don't have a *choice,*" Anna said, just as quietly but with steel behind the softness. "We're stuck without a car or food, we don't have anywhere to sleep. . . . Listen to me, Rob. My parents can take care of themselves. Right now *we're* the ones in trouble."

"She's right," Lewis said soberly. "What else can we do? We can't afford a hotel and we can't sleep out here."

Rob nodded reluctantly. Kaitlyn allowed herself to feel some relief. Just the thought of having somewhere specific to go was comforting. But Anna's next words dispelled the comfort.

"It means we'll have to give up following the coast,"

Anna was saying. "We should just cut straight across to the Sound. We'll have to hitchhike, I guess."

"Five of us?" Gabriel said. "Who's going to pick up five teenagers?"

Secretly Kaitlyn agreed. Standing in the rain trying to get a ride—in a strange state—when there were five of you—and you had to be on the alert for the police . . . well, it wasn't her idea of fun. But what other choice did they have?

"We've got to try," Rob was saying. "At least, maybe somebody will take Anna and Kait with 'em— and then maybe the girls can find a phone and call Anna's folks."

Helping each other, they climbed through the wet ferns and bracken, up the embankment, and to the road. Rob said they had better walk a little distance away from the van to lessen the chance that they'd be connected with it.

"We're lucky," he said. "You can't see the creek from the road, and nobody was around to actually see the accident."

Kaitlyn tried to keep reminding herself she was lucky as she stuck her thumb out, staring down the lonely road.

There weren't many cars. A long truck carrying huge logs passed without stopping. So did a black Chevy pickup full of orange and green fishing net.

Kaitlyn looked around as they waited. The rain had eased to a drizzle, but the world had a sodden look that was rather menacing. All the trees here, including the alders, were covered with thick mint-colored moss. It was a disturbing sight, all those branches that weren't white or brown, but lumpy unnatural green.

She felt a glow in the web just as Lewis asked, "What are you doing, Rob?"

Rob was standing with his eyes shut, an expression of concentration on his face. "Just moving energy around," he said. "I could think better if this cut would start healing." He opened his eyes, pulling the T-shirt bandage off. Kait saw with relief that the cut had stopped bleeding. There was even a little color in Rob's face.

"Okay," he said and smiled. "Now, how about the rest of you? Anybody starting to hurt?"

Lewis shrugged; Anna shook her head. Gabriel kept looking down the road, ignoring the question.

Kaitlyn shifted, then said, "No, I'm fine." She wasn't; she was chilled and miserable and her entire left side had begun to ache. But she felt somehow that she didn't merit healing. She didn't *deserve* it.

"Kait—I can *feel* you're not," Rob was beginning, when Lewis said, "Another car!"

It was approaching slowly, an old Pontiac the color of pumpkin pie.

"It won't stop," Gabriel said sourly. "Nobody's going to stop for five teenagers."

The car passed them, and Kait got a glimpse of a young woman behind the rain-splattered window. Then brake lights flashed, and the car slowed to a stop.

"Come on!" Rob said.

As they reached the car, the driver's window opened. Kaitlyn heard the beat of Caribbean music, and then a voice. "You looking for a ride?"

It wasn't a young woman, Kaitlyn realized. It was a girl. A girl who didn't look any older than they were. She was slender and small-boned, with a pale and delicate face that contrasted sharply with her heavy shock of dark hair. Her eyes were gray-green.

"We sure are," Lewis said eagerly. Kaitlyn could feel his admiration in the web. "We're a little wet, though," he added apologetically. "Well, more than a little. A lot."

"Doesn't matter," the girl said carelessly. "The seats are vinyl—it's my granny's car. Get in."

Kaitlyn hesitated. There was something about this girl—she seemed fragile, but there was something almost furtive about her.

Rob? I'm not sure we should.

Rob glanced at Kait in surprise. *What's wrong?*

I don't know. She's just—does she seem okay to you?

She seems great *to me,* Lewis interrupted. *Jeez, what a babe. And I'm freezing out here.*

Kaitlyn still wasn't sure. *Anna?*

Anna had been walking around the back of the Pontiac, but had stopped at Kaitlyn's first message. Now she said gently, *You're probably still shaken up, Kait. I think she's fine—and besides, we can all fit in this car!*

"Yes, we can, can't we?" Gabriel said aloud, not seeming to mind the girl's inquisitive glance. Kaitlyn wondered how they must appear to the girl—all five of them standing frozen and silent—and then Gabriel suddenly coming out with this strange rhetorical question.

All right, let's do it, Kait said hastily. She was embarrassed, and she didn't want to argue anymore. But as Rob opened the door, she asked Gabriel, *What did you mean?*

Nothing. It's just an interesting coincidence that we fit, that's all.

Anna and Lewis got in the front with the girl. Kaitlyn slid in the back seat after Rob, and Gabriel followed her. The white vinyl seats creaked under their weight.

"My name's Lydia," the girl said in that same careless voice. "Where are you going?"

They introduced themselves—or rather Lewis introduced them—and Anna said, "We're trying to get to Suquamish, near Poulsbo—but that's pretty far away. Where were you headed?"

Lydia shrugged. "I wasn't headed anywhere, really. I took the day off school to drive around."

"Oh, do you go to North Mason High? I have a cousin there."

Anna's question was perfectly innocent, but Lydia seemed affronted. "It's a private school," she said briefly. Then she said, "Are you getting enough heat back there? If I turn it too high, the windows steam up."

"It feels great," Rob said. He was holding Kaitlyn's hands in his own, rubbing them. And he was right, being in a warm dry car was wonderful. Kaitlyn's brain felt almost stupefied at the sudden luxury.

She was aware, though, that Lydia was watching them keenly, casting glances at Lewis and Anna beside her, then looking up into the rearview mirror to examine the three in the back. Although Lewis seemed to enjoy the scrutiny it made Kait uncomfortable, particularly when Lydia began frowning and chewing her lip in a speculative way.

"So what were you doing back there?" Lydia asked finally, very casually. "You're awfully wet."

"Oh. We were . . ." Lewis fumbled for words.

"We went for a hike," Gabriel said evenly. "We got caught in the rain."

"Looks more like you got caught in a flood."

"We found a creek," Gabriel said before Lewis could answer.

"So you guys are from around here?"

"From Suquamish," Anna said—and for her, at least, that was the truth.

"You take long hikes," Lydia said, looking in the rearview mirror again. Kait noticed that she had exactly three freckles on her small nose.

Somehow Lydia's skepticism had calmed Kait's own suspicions. It wasn't really furtiveness lurking in those gray-green eyes, she decided. It was more defensiveness, as if Lydia had been beaten up by life a great deal. Kaitlyn felt sympathetic.

They were driving inland, now, through stands of evergreen trees with tall bare trunks. To Kaitlyn, they looked like hundreds of soldiers standing at attention.

Lydia shook back her hair and tilted her chin up. "I hate going to private school," she said suddenly. "My parents make me."

Kaitlyn, relaxing in the warmth of the car, tried to think of something to say to that. But Lewis was already sympathizing. "That's too bad."

"It's so strict—and boring. Nothing exciting ever happens."

"I know. I went to private school once," Lewis said. Lydia changed the subject abruptly.

"Do you always take duffel bags when you go hiking?"

"Yes," Gabriel said. He seemed to be able to handle Lydia best. "We use them like backpacks," he said, seeming amused.

"Isn't that a little awkward?"

Gabriel didn't answer. Lewis just smiled engagingly.

There was another minute or so of fidgeting from Lydia, and then she burst out, "You're running away, aren't you? You don't really live around here at all. You're hitchhiking across the country or something—aren't you?"

Don't tell her anything, Gabriel thought to Lewis, just as Lydia said, "You don't have to tell me. I don't care. But I wish *I* could have an adventure sometime. I'm so tired of private riding clubs and country clubs and Key Clubs and the Assistance League." She was silent for a moment and then added, "I'll drive you to Suquamish if you'll tell me the way. I don't care how far it is."

Kaitlyn didn't know what to make of the girl. She was a strange, excitable creature—that was certain. And she felt left out, an outsider looking in on the five of them.

Kaitlyn remembered how that felt—being outside. Back in Ohio she had been outside everything. She'd been too different; her blue-ringed eyes had been too strange, her psychic drawings had been too spooky. No one at her old high school had wanted to consort with the local witch.

But she still wasn't sure about Lydia—and she didn't like the way Lydia pushed so hard to get in.

Don't tell her anything, she advised Lewis, echoing Gabriel's opinion. After a moment Lewis lifted his shoulders in acquiescence.

"We'd be grateful if you'd take us to Suquamish," Rob said gently, and then they all shut up and listened to the radio.

"Turn here," Anna said. "It's just down this street —there, that house with the Oldsmobile in front of it."

It was twilight, but Kaitlyn could see that the house was the same red-brown color as Anna's cedar basket. It must be made of cedar, she realized. The spruce and alder trees around it were becoming mere towering shapes as dark fell.

"We're here," Anna said softly.

A house, Kaitlyn thought. A real house with parents in it, adults who would help take care of them. For the moment it was all Kait wanted. She stretched her stiff, clammy legs and watched Gabriel reach for the door handle.

Lydia blurted, "I guess you weren't running away. I didn't know you really had somewhere to go. Sorry."

"It doesn't matter. Thanks for the ride," Rob said.

Lydia hunched her shoulders. "Sure," she said. It was the voice of someone who hasn't been invited to a party. Then she said in subdued tones, "Could I use your bathroom?"

"Oh—sure," Anna said. "Hang on, I'd better go inside first." *Mom isn't going to be expecting us,* she added silently.

Moving quickly and lightly, Anna ran up to the house. The others waited in the car, looking through steam-clouded windows. After a few minutes Anna came back, leading a short, motherly woman who looked bewildered but humorously resigned. Kait thought suddenly that she knew where Anna got her serenity.

"Come inside, all of you," the woman said. "I'm Mrs. Whiteraven, Anna's mother. Oh, my goodness, you're wet and half-frozen. Come in!"

They went in, and Lydia went with them.

Inside, Kaitlyn got a quick impression of a crowded, comfortable living room and two identical boys who looked about nine or ten. Then Anna's mother was hustling them into the back of the house, running hot baths and gathering clean clothes.

"You boys will just have to wear some of my husband's things," she said. "They'll be big, but they'll have to do."

Some time later Kaitlyn found herself warm and faintly damp from a bath, dressed in Anna's clothes and sitting in front of the fireplace.

"Your mother's nice," she whispered to Anna. "Isn't she a little surprised to have us turn up like this? Did she ask you any questions?"

Not yet. She's more interested in feeding us and getting us warm. But I know one thing—she hasn't heard anything from the Institute. She thought I was still at school.

They had to stop talking then because Anna's little brothers came in and started asking her about California. Anna managed to tell them about it without mentioning Mr. Zetes or the Institute.

Mrs. Whiteraven bustled back in. "Anna, your other friend was just waiting in the hall. I sent her to wash up. We'll have dinner in a few minutes, as soon as the boys are ready."

"But she isn't—" Anna began. She broke off as Lydia walked into the room, looking small and almost pathetic. It would be too rude to say "she isn't my friend" when Mrs. Whiteraven had just invited her to dinner.

After all, she did give us a ride, Anna said to Kaitlyn, who shrugged.

Rob, Gabriel, and Lewis appeared wearing billowing flannel shirts and jeans tightly belted to keep them on. Kaitlyn and Anna nobly refrained from giggling, but Lydia grinned. Lewis grinned back at her, unabashed. They sat down with Anna's mother and father at the table.

Dinner was hamburgers and smoked salmon, corn and broccoli and salad, with berry pie for dessert and Thomas Kemper's Old Fashioned Birch Soda to wash it down. Kaitlyn had never been so happy to see vegetables. All five of them from the Institute dug in with an enthusiasm that made Mrs. Whiteraven's eyes widen, but she didn't ask any questions until they'd finished eating.

Then she wiped her hands on a dish towel, pushed her chair back, and said, "Now, suppose you kids explain what you're doing in Washington?"

11

Kaitlyn looked from Anna's mother to Anna's father, a grave man with steady eyes who'd scarcely spoken during dinner. The kitchen was warm and quiet. Yellow light shone from the overhead lamp onto unfinished pine cupboards.

Then Kaitlyn looked at Rob. They were all looking at one another, all five who shared the web.

Should we? Anna asked.

Yes, Kaitlyn thought back, feeling agreement from the others. *But only your parents. Not . . .*

Anna waved a hand at her twin brothers. "You guys go play, okay? And . . ." She glanced at Lydia and faltered. Kaitlyn knew the problem; Anna was gentle by nature, and it was difficult to say "get out" to a guest who'd just eaten at the same table.

You're too soft-hearted, she thought, but Gabriel was already speaking.

"Maybe Lydia and I could take a walk outside," he

said. "It's stopped raining now." Standing, he looked every inch the gallant gentleman—if you didn't count the mocking glint in his eyes. He extended his hand to Lydia courteously.

There wasn't much Lydia could do. She went rather pale, so that her three freckles stood out more prominently. Then she thanked Anna's parents and took Gabriel's hand. Lewis gave her a hurt look.

Be careful, Kaitlyn thought to Gabriel as he and Lydia walked out.

Of what? Psychic attacks—or her? he sent back, amused.

Anna's brothers went, too. And then there was no further excuse for delay. With one final look at her mind-mates, Anna took a deep breath and began telling her parents the whole story.

Almost the whole story. She left out some of the more gruesome bits and didn't mention the mind-link at all. But she told about Marisol, and the crystal that enhanced psychic power, and Mr. Zetes's plans for making his students into a psychic strike team. Rob went and got the files he'd taken from the hidden room.

"And we've been having these dreams," Anna said. "About a little peninsula with gray water all around it, and across from it is a cliff with trees and a white house. And we think that the people in the house might be sending us the dreams, trying to help us." She told about Kaitlyn's two encounters with the caramel-skinned man who came from the white house.

"He didn't seem to like the Institute," Kait put in.

"And he showed me a picture of a garden with a huge crystal in it—like Mr. Z's crystal. We figure that maybe they know about these things."

Mrs. Whiteraven frowned. Her black eyes had been snapping and flashing throughout Anna's story, especially when Anna told about Mr. Z's plans. Mr. Whiteraven had merely gotten more and more grave-looking, one of his hands slowly clenching into a fist. Like Tony, they seemed to have no trouble accepting the reality of what Anna was saying.

Now Anna's mother spoke. "But—you're saying you set out for this white house without any idea where it is?"

"We have *some* idea," Anna said. "It's north. And we'll know it when we see it—the peninsula is lined with these strange rock piles. I keep thinking they're familiar somehow. They look like this." She got a pencil and began drawing on the back of one of the file folders. "No—Kait, you're the artist. Draw one."

Kaitlyn did her best, sketching one of the tall, irregular rock stacks. It came out looking a bit like a stone snowman with outspread arms.

"Oh, it's an *inuk shuk*," Mrs. Whiteraven said.

Kaitlyn's head jerked up. "You *recognize* it?"

Anna's mother turned the paper, studying it. "Yes —I'm sure it's an *inuk shuk*. The Inuit used them for signals, you know, to show that a certain place was friendly or that visitors were welcome—"

"The *Inuit?*" Anna interrupted, choking. "You mean we have to go to Alaska?"

Her mother waved a hand, brow puckering. "I'm sure I've seen some of these much closer. . . . I know!

133

It was somewhere on Vancouver Island. We took a trip there when you were about five or six. Yes, and I'm sure we saw them there."

Everyone began talking at once.

"Vancouver Island—that's Canada—" Rob said.

"Yes, but it's not far—there's a ferry," Anna said. "No *wonder* those things were familiar—"

"I've never been to Canada," said Lewis.

"But do you remember exactly *where* they were?" Kaitlyn was asking Mrs. Whiteraven.

"No, dear, I'm afraid not. It was a long time ago." Anna's mother chewed her lip gently, frowning at the picture. Then she sighed and shook her head.

"It doesn't matter," Rob said. His eyes were alight with excitement. "At least we know the general area. And somebody on the island has *got* to know where they are. We'll just keep asking."

Anna's mother put the paper down. "Now, just a minute," she said. She and her husband exchanged a glance.

Kaitlyn, looking from one of them to the other, had a sudden sinking feeling.

"Now," Mrs. Whiteraven said, turning away from her husband. "You kids have been very brave and resourceful so far. But this idea about finding the white house—it's not practical. This isn't a problem for children."

"No," said Mr. Whiteraven. He'd been looking through the files Rob had brought. "It's a problem for the authorities. There's enough proof here to get your Mr. Zetes put away for a long time."

"But you don't understand how powerful he is," Anna said. "He's got friends everywhere. And

Marisol's brother said that only magic could fight magic—"

"I hardly think Marisol's brother is an expert," her mother said tartly. "You should have gone to your parents in the first place. And that reminds me, you have to *call* your parents, now—all of you."

Kait hardened herself. "We can't tell them anything that would make them feel better. And if Mr. Zetes has some way of tapping the call—well, he'd know exactly where we are."

"If he doesn't already," Anna said softly.

"But . . ." Mrs. Whiteraven sighed and exchanged another look with her husband. "All right, *I'll* call them in the morning. I don't need to tell them exactly where you are until we get this thing straightened out."

"Straightened out how, ma'am?" Rob asked. His eyes had darkened.

"We'll talk to the elders, then to the police," Anna's mother said firmly. "That's the right thing to do."

Anna opened her mouth, then shut it again. *It's no good,* she told the others helplessly.

No. It isn't, Rob agreed.

Lewis said, *Jeeeez. I guess we should be relieved, but*—

Kaitlyn knew what he meant. Adults were in the picture now, taking charge, handling things. The authorities were going to be told. The five of them didn't have to worry anymore. She should have been happy.

So why did her chest feel so tight?

Two thoughts jostled in her brain. One was: After we got so far . . .

The other was: The adults don't know Mr. Z.

"Now we'll have to find places for you to sleep," Anna's mother was saying briskly. "You two boys can have the twins' room, and I'll put your friend Gabriel on the couch. Then Anna can share her room with you, Kait, and Lydia can go in the guest room—"

"Lydia's not sleeping here," Kaitlyn blurted, before thinking about how rude this sounded. "She's not one of us; she just gave us a ride."

Mrs. Whiteraven looked surprised. "Well, you can't expect her to drive all the way home now. It's too late, and she told me before dinner that she was tired. I've already invited her to stay overnight."

Kaitlyn started to groan, then realized that Rob and Anna and especially Lewis were looking at her reproachfully. In the web she could feel their bewilderment—they didn't understand what she had against Lydia.

Oh, well, what difference did it make anyway? Kait shrugged and bent her head.

Gabriel and Lydia came strolling through the door a few minutes later. Lydia didn't look particularly disappointed to have missed the kitchen conference. She kept glancing up at Gabriel through her lashes—a stratagem that seemed to amuse Gabriel and annoy Lewis. Kait and Anna left Rob to fill Gabriel in on what had happened while they helped make up the guest room bed.

So the quest is over? Gabriel asked. Kaitlyn could hear him perfectly even though he was in the kitchen and she was giving a final punch to Lydia's pillow.

We'll talk about it tomorrow, she told him grimly. She was tired.

136

And she was worried about Gabriel. Again. Still. She could tell that he was in pain—she could feel the tension shimmering under his surface. But somehow she didn't think he was going to let her help tonight.

He didn't. He wouldn't talk about it, either, not even when she managed to sneak a moment alone with him while the others were getting ready for bed.

"But what are you going to do?" She had dreadful visions of him sneaking into Anna's parents' room, too crazed to know what he was doing.

"Nothing," he said shortly, and then, with icy fury, "I'm a *guest* here."

So he'd caught her vision. And he had his own code of honor. But that didn't mean he could hold out all night. . . .

He was already walking away.

Kaitlyn climbed into Anna's double bed feeling uneasy and discouraged.

It was just dawn when she woke. She found herself staring at the luminous green numbers on Anna's clock radio, a knot twisting in her stomach. She could sense the others sleeping—even Gabriel. He was so restless that she could tell he hadn't been out anywhere.

Strangely, of all the things she had to worry about, the one bothering her was Lydia.

Forget Lydia, she told herself. But her mind kept spinning out the same questions. Who was Lydia, and why was she so eager to be with them? What was wrong with the girl? And why did Kait keep feeling she wasn't to be trusted?

There should be some way to tell, Kait thought. Some test or something. . . .

Kait sat up.

Then, quickly but as stealthily as possible, she slid out of bed and picked up her duffel bag. She took the bag into the bathroom and locked the door.

With the light on she fished through the bag until she found her art kit. The sealed Tupperware had survived the creek, and her pastels and erasers were safe. The sketchpad was damp, though.

Oh, well. Oil pastels didn't mind the damp. Kaitlyn picked up a black pastel stick, held it poised over the blank page, and shut her eyes.

She'd never done this before; trying to *make* a picture come when she didn't already feel the need to draw. Now she made use of some of Joyce's techniques, deliberately relaxing and shutting out the world.

Clear your mind. Now think of Lydia. Think of drawing Lydia. . . . Let the picture come. . . .

Black lines radiating downward. Kaitlyn saw the image and let her hand transfer it to the paper. Now some black grape mixed in. Blue for highlights—it was Lydia's hair. Then pale fleshtones for Lydia's face and celadon green for Lydia's eyes.

But she felt she needed the black again. Heavy strokes of black, lots of them, above and around Lydia's portrait, forming a silhouette that seemed to be cradling Lydia, encompassing her.

Kaitlyn's eyes opened all the way, and she stared at the drawing. That broad-shouldered silhouette with body lines that swept straight down like a man in a coat . . .

In one furious motion she was on her feet.

I'll kill her. Oh, my God, I'm going to *kill* her. . . .

She jerked open the bathroom door and headed for the guest room.

Lydia was a slender shape under the covers. Kait turned her over and grabbed her by the throat.

Lydia made a noise like Georgie Mouse. Her eyes showed white in the darkness.

"You nasty, spying, sneaking little *weasel,*" Kait said and shook her a few times. She spoke softly, so as not to wake Anna's parents, and put most of her energy into the shaking.

Lydia made more noises. Kaitlyn thought she was trying to say, "What are you talking about?"

"I'll tell you what I'm talking about," she said, punctuating each word with a shake. Lydia was gripping her wrists with both hands, but was too weak to break Kait's hold. "You're working for Mr. Zetes, you little worm."

Squeaking feebly, Lydia tried to shake her head.

"Yes, you are! I *know* it. I'm psychic, remember?"

As Kaitlyn finished speaking, she sensed activity behind her. It was her mind-mates, crowding in the doorway. So much emotion, so close, had gotten through to all of them even in their sleep.

"Hey! What are you doing?" Lewis was saying in alarm, and Rob said, "Kait, what's happening? You woke everybody up. . . ."

Kaitlyn barely turned. "She's a spy!"

"What?" Charming in too-big pajamas, Rob came to stand beside the bed. When he saw Kaitlyn's grip on Lydia's throat, he reached instinctively. Lewis was right behind him.

"Don't, you guys. She's a spy—aren't you?" Kaitlyn tried to bang Lydia's head against the headboard, but didn't have enough leverage.

"Hey!"

"Kait, just calm down—"

"Admit it!" Kait told the struggling Lydia. "Admit it and I'll let you go!"

Just as Rob was putting his arms around Kait, trying to pull her away, Lydia nodded.

Kaitlyn let go. "I did a drawing that showed she's working for Mr. Zetes," she said to Rob. To Lydia, she added, "Tell them!"

Lydia was coughing and choking, trying to get enough air. Finally she managed to wheeze, "I'm a spy."

Rob dropped his arms, and Lewis looked almost comically dismayed. "What?"

A wave of ugly emotion came from Gabriel. Images of Lydia being chopped into little pieces and thrown in the ocean. Kaitlyn winced and for the first time realized that her hands were sore.

The others had gathered around the bed now. Anna was somber, and Lewis looked hurt and betrayed. Rob crossed his arms over his chest.

"All right," he said to Lydia. "Start talking."

Lydia sat up, small and ghostly in her white nightgown. She looked at each of the five rather threatening figures surrounding her bed.

"I am a spy," she said. "But I'm not working for Mr. Zetes."

"Oh, come off it," Kaitlyn said, and Gabriel said, "Of course you're not," in his silkiest, most sinister manner.

"I'm *not*. I don't work for him. . . . I'm his daughter."

Kaitlyn felt her jaw sag. Unbelievable—but, wait. Joyce *had* mentioned that Mr. Zetes had a daughter. . . .

She said the daughter was friends with Marisol, Rob agreed.

Kaitlyn remembered. She also remembered thinking that any daughter of Mr. Zetes's would have to be old, strangely old to be friends with Marisol.

"How old are you?" she said suspiciously to Lydia.

"Eighteen last month. Look, if you don't believe me, my driver's license is in my purse."

Gabriel picked a black Chanel purse off the floor and dumped its contents on the bed, ignoring Lydia's murmur of protest. He extracted a wallet.

"Lydia Zetes," he said, and showed the driver's license to the others.

"How did you *get* here?" Rob demanded.

Lydia blinked and swallowed. She was either on the verge of tears or an excellent actress, Kaitlyn thought. "I flew. On a plane."

"The astral plane?" Gabriel asked. He was very angry.

"On a *jet*," Lydia said. "My father sent me, and I got the car from a friend of his, a director of Boeing. My father called and told me where you'd be—"

"Which he knew because he set up a trap for us," Rob interrupted, seizing on this. "A trap with a goat. He knew if we didn't get killed in the accident, we'd be stranded—"

"Yes. And I was supposed to come along and help you—if any of you were still alive."

141

"You—little—" Words failed Kaitlyn. She grabbed for Lydia's throat again, but Gabriel was faster.

"Don't bother with it. *I'll* take care of her," he said. Kaitlyn sensed cold hunger.

Everyone in the web knew what he meant. The interesting thing was that *Lydia* seemed to know what he meant, too. She flinched, scooting back against the headboard.

"You don't understand! I'm not your enemy," she said in a voice laced with raw panic.

"Sure you're not," Lewis said.

"No, you're just his daughter," said Kaitlyn. Then she felt Anna's hand on her arm.

"Wait a minute," Anna said quietly. "At least let her say what she wants to." To Lydia, she said, softly but severely, "Go on."

Lydia gulped and addressed herself to Anna. "I know you won't believe me, but what I told you in the car was true. I *do* hate private school, and riding clubs, and country clubs. And I hate my father. All I ever wanted was to get away—"

"Yeah, yeah," Lewis said. Gabriel just laughed.

"It's *true,*" Lydia said fiercely. "I hate what he does to people. I didn't want to come after you, but it was my only chance."

Something about her voice made Lewis falter in his sneering. Kaitlyn could feel his indecision in the web.

"You weren't going to tell us, though, were you?" Kaitlyn said. "You'd never have told us who you were if I hadn't found out."

"I *was* going to," Lydia said. She squirmed. "I *wanted* to," she amended. "But I knew you wouldn't believe me."

"Oh, stop sniveling," Gabriel said.

Kaitlyn was looking at Rob. *I know I'm going to hate myself for asking this—but do you think it could be true?*

I . . . don't know. Rob grinned suddenly. *But maybe we can find out.*

He sat on the bed, taking Lydia by the shoulders, and looked into her face. She shrank back.

"Now listen to me," he said sternly. "You know that we're psychics, right? Well, Kaitlyn has the power to tell if you're lying or not." To Kait he said, *Go get your drawing stuff.*

Kaitlyn hid a smile and brought it from the bathroom. Rob went on, "All she has to do is make a drawing. And if that drawing says you're not telling the truth . . ." He shook his head darkly. "Now," he said, looking hard at Lydia again, "what's your story this time?"

Lydia looked at Kait, then at Rob. She lifted her chin. "It's the same. Everything I told you was true," she said steadily.

Kaitlyn made a few scribbles on the pad. Her gift didn't work that way, of course, but she knew that the real test here was of Lydia's demeanor.

Well? she asked Rob.

Either she's telling the truth or she's the greatest actress in the world.

Like Joyce? Gabriel put in pointedly. *You know, I could probably tell if she's telling the truth. I could mind-link with her.*

Yeah, but what are the chances that she'd survive? Rob asked.

Gabriel shrugged. The hunger flickered again.

"Look, what was it you were supposed to do when you found us?" Kaitlyn asked Lydia.

"Keep you guys from going wherever you were going," she said promptly. "Convince you to go to the police or something instead—"

"He *wants* that? Your father?"

"Oh, yes. He knows he can fix the police. He's got lots of friends, and he can do things with the crystal. He's not afraid of police; he's afraid of *them.*"

"Who?" Kaitlyn demanded.

"Them. The people of the crystal. He doesn't know where they are, but he's afraid you'll find them. They're the only ones who can stop him." She looked around. "*Now* do you believe me? Would I have told you that if I were your enemy?"

Kaitlyn could feel the wavering in the web, and the sudden resolution. Rob and Anna believed her. Lewis not only believed her but liked her again. Gabriel was cynical, but that was typical Gabriel. And Kait herself was convinced enough to have a new worry.

"If Mr. Z *wants* us to go to the police—" she began.

"Right," Rob said grimly.

"But we'll never convince my parents," Anna said.

"Right," Rob said again.

A feeling was stirring in Kaitlyn, part terror, part dismay, and part wild excitement.

Lewis gulped. "But that means—"

"Right," Rob said a third time. He grinned at Kait, his grin reflecting her bewildering mix of emotions. "The search," he announced to the room at large, "is back on."

Gabriel cursed.

Lydia was looking from one of them to another in bewilderment. "I don't understand."

"It means we're going to have to run away again," Rob said. "And if you really want to help us—"

"I do."

"—you can drive us to Vancouver Island. There's a ferry, right?" He glanced at Anna, who nodded.

"I'll do it," Lydia said simply. "When do we go?"

"Right *now*," Kaitlyn said. "We've got to get out of here before Anna's parents wake up."

"Okay, everybody," Rob said. "Grab your things and let's get moving."

12

The ferry leaves from Port Angeles at eight-twenty," Anna said as she and Kaitlyn hurriedly changed their clothes in her bedroom.

"It's started raining again," said Kaitlyn.

They all met a few minutes later in the front hallway. There were ominous stirring noises from the back of the house.

"Shouldn't you leave a note?" Lewis whispered.

Anna sighed. "They'll know," she said briefly.

"I'll leave them the files," Rob said. "Maybe they can do something with them."

Gabriel snorted.

Outside, the sky was cold and gray. The rain seemed to come at them horizontally as they drove to Port Angeles. If they kept the defroster on maximum, it cleared the windshield but scorched their skin; if they turned it down, the windshield immediately steamed over. If they opened the windows, it cleared everything but they froze.

146

At the ferry the water was navy blue with just a hint of green. They waited in a line of cars and finally drove onto a large boat. It cost twenty-five dollars, and Kaitlyn paid because Lydia only had credit cards.

On the passenger deck Kaitlyn watched the deep blue water slipping away on either side. We're on our way, she thought. To Canada. She had never been to a foreign country.

She was drinking a vending-machine Coke that Rob had brought her when Lewis rushed up, breathless.

"Trouble," he said. "I just talked to some kids in the bathroom. They said if you're under eighteen, you're supposed to have a letter of authorization to get into Canada."

"What?"

"A letter. From your parents or something, I guess. Telling who you are and how long you're going to be there."

"Oh, *terrific.*" Kaitlyn looked at Rob, who shrugged.

"What can we do? We'll just hope they don't ask for one."

"I'm eighteen, anyway," Lydia said. "I'll drive and maybe the rest of you can fake it."

An hour later they cruised into Victoria Harbor. Kaitlyn's breath caught. The sun had come out, and the harbor was a picture begging to be painted. There were lots of little sailboats and lots of clean-looking pink and white buildings.

But she couldn't keep staring; they had to go downstairs again and get in the car. They waited in another line at the customs checkpoint while the knot in Kaitlyn's stomach wound tighter and tighter.

"Where do you live?" a sunglassed customs officer asked Lydia.

Lydia's fingers barely tightened on the wheel. "In California," she said, smiling.

The customs officer didn't smile back. He asked to see Lydia's driver's license. He asked where they were going in Canada and how long they'd be staying. Lydia answered everything in a careless, sophisticated murmur. Then the officer bent a little at the waist to examine the inside of the car.

Look old, Kaitlyn told the others. They all sat up straight and tried to look mature and bored.

The customs officer didn't change expression. He glanced at each of them, then straightened.

"Any of you under eighteen?" he asked Lydia.

Kaitlyn's stomach gave a final sickening twist. Their driver's licenses would show the rest of them were *all* under eighteen. And then he'd ask for a letter. . . .

Lydia hesitated imperceptibly. Then she said "Oh, no." She said it lightly, with something like a toss of her head. Kaitlyn admired that. Although Lydia was slight, her manner was sophisticated and assured.

The customs officer hesitated. He was looking at Lewis—the one of them who looked youngest. Lydia glanced back at Lewis, too, and although her face was calm, her gaze was almost desperate. Pleading. Lewis's jaw set, and Kaitlyn felt a ripple in the web.

The customs officer had something hanging at his belt, a pager or walkie-talkie or something. Suddenly it began to shriek.

Not beep. *Wail.* It went off with a sound like an air-raid siren, a vibrating sound that put Kaitlyn's teeth on edge. People turned to look.

The customs officer was shaking the walkie-talkie, pressing buttons. The shrieking only went up in volume.

The officer looked from the device to the car as if hesitating. Then he grimaced, trying to muffle the electronic shrilling. With an impatient hand, he waved Lydia on.

"Go, go," Lewis whispered excitedly.

Lydia put the car in gear, and they glided off at a majestic five miles an hour. When they reached a main street, Kaitlyn let out her breath. They'd made it!

"Easier than I thought," Rob said.

In the back seat Lewis was chortling. "How about that? One for the home team!"

Kaitlyn turned on him. That ripple she'd felt in the web just before the shrieking began . . . "Lewis—did *you?*"

Lewis's grin widened, his eyes sparkling. "I figured if those creeps could sabotage us with long distance PK, I could handle a walkie-talkie. I just made a few little adjustments to give it some feedback."

Lydia glanced back at him again, and for the first time there was something like appreciation in her gray-green eyes. "Thanks," she said. "You saved my you-know-what." Lewis beamed.

Even Gabriel seemed grudgingly impressed. But he asked Lydia smoothly, "Who are those creeps, by the way? The ones who've been trying to kill us with psychic attacks."

"I don't know. Truly, I *don't*. I know my father has been doing something with the crystal—and he may have people helping him. But I don't know who."

"I wonder if they've stopped," Anna said suddenly. "I mean, there wasn't an attack last night. Maybe they've lost track of us."

"And maybe they're relying on somebody else to keep track," Gabriel said, with a meaningful look at Lydia. She gave something very much like a flounce without interfering with her driving.

"Where am I supposed to go now?" she asked.

There was a pause. Then Rob said, "We're not sure."

"You came here without knowing where you're *going?*"

"We don't know exactly. We're looking for—"

"Something," Gabriel said, interrupting Rob. Lewis frowned and Kaitlyn gave Gabriel an impatient look.

We decided to trust her. And she's going to find out anyway, as soon as we find it. . . .

"Then let her wait until we find it," Gabriel said aloud. "Why trust any further than we have to?"

Lydia's lips tightened, but she didn't say anything, and she didn't flounce again.

"I figure we have two choices," Rob said. "We can drive up and down the coast blindly, or we can *ask* people around here if they know where the—" He changed for an instant to silent speech: *the rock towers are.* "If Anna's mom recognized them, people on the island should know them."

"Can't *you* remember anything, Anna?" Lewis asked. "Your mom said you were on that trip, too."

"I was five," Anna said.

They decided to ask around. A man at a tourist shop sold them a map and directed them to the Royal

British Columbia Museum. But although the museum people recognized Kaitlyn's sketch of an *inuk shuk,* they had no idea where any might be found on the island. Neither did anyone at the camera shop, or the bookstore, or the British imports store, or the native crafts shop. Neither did the librarians at the Victoria Library.

"Is it time to start driving around blindly?" Gabriel asked.

Lewis pulled out the map.

"We can drive either northeast or northwest," he said. "This island's sort of like a big oval and we're at the bottom. And before you ask, *nothing* on here looks like our Griffin's Pit. There're thousands of little peninsulas and things all over the coast, and no way to tell any of them apart."

"It's probably too small to be on the map, anyway," Rob said. "Flip a coin: Heads we go east, tails we go west."

Kaitlyn flipped a coin and it came up heads.

They drove northeast, following the coastline, stopping to check the ocean every few miles. They drove until it was dark, but they found nothing resembling the place in their dream.

"But the ocean is right," Anna said, standing on a rock and looking down into the blue-gray water. Gulls were crowded thickly around her—they took off when Kaitlyn or the others came near, but tolerated Anna as if she were a bird.

"It's *almost* right," Kaitlyn temporized. "Maybe we need to go farther north, or to try going west." It was frustrating to feel she was so close to the place, but not to be able to sense where it was.

"Well, we're not going to find anything tonight," Gabriel said. "The light's gone."

Kaitlyn heard the note of tension in his voice. Not just ordinary Gabriel-tension, but a fine edge that told her he was in trouble.

All day he'd been quieter than usual, withdrawn, as if he were wrapping himself around his private pain. His control was getting better, but his need was getting worse. It had been nearly thirty-six hours since Kaitlyn had caught him on the beach in Oregon.

And what on earth is he going to do tonight? Kaitlyn wondered.

"I beg your pardon?" Rob said, looking at her quickly.

She'd forgotten to screen her thoughts. Desperately hoping he'd only caught the last bit, she said, "I was wondering what on earth we're going to do tonight. To sleep, I mean. We're almost broke—"

"And starving," Lewis put in.

"—and we certainly can't all sleep in this car."

"We'll have to find a cheap motel," Anna said. "We can afford one room, anyway, since it's off season. We'd better head back for Victoria."

In Victoria they found the Sitka Spruce Inn, which let them have a room with two twin beds for thirty-eight dollars and didn't ask any questions. The paint inside the room was peeling and the door to the bathroom didn't shut properly, but, as Anna pointed out, it did have beds.

At Rob's direction the girls got the beds. Lydia chose to share with Anna—clearly she hadn't forgotten the strangling. Kaitlyn curled up on the other, pulling the thin coverlet over her. The boys, sleeping on the carpet, had usurped the blankets.

She slept, but lightly. All that evening Gabriel had avoided her, refused to speak with her. Kait could tell by his cold determination that he was bent on solving his problem alone—and she didn't think that he was going to lie there and quietly endure it again tonight. By now she was closely enough attuned to him that she thought she'd wake up when he did.

It worked—mostly. Kaitlyn woke when the hotel door closed with a click. She could sense that Gabriel wasn't in the room.

Getting out of bed stealthily was almost routine now. The only shock came when Kaitlyn looked at the other bed and realized that there was only one figure in it.

Lydia was gone. Not in the bathroom, either. Just gone.

Kaitlyn crept out of the room feeling very grim.

She tracked Gabriel by his presence in the web, feeling him move away from her, following. She wondered if Lydia was with him.

Eventually she came out by the harbor.

Kaitlyn hadn't been afraid walking down the quaint, old-fashioned streets of Victoria. There were a few people out, and an atmosphere of sleepy safety blanketed the town. But here by the harbor it was very quiet, very lonely. The lights of boats and buildings reflected in the water, but it was still dark and the wharf was deserted.

She found Gabriel pacing in the shadows.

He looked something like a wild animal, a captured

predator pacing out the confines of his cage. As Kaitlyn got closer, she could sense the intensity of his hunger.

"Where's Lydia?" she said.

He swung around to stare at her. "Can't you leave me alone?"

"Are you alone?"

There was no sound but the soft swish of water for a moment. Then Gabriel said with careful precision, "I have no idea where Lydia is. I came out by myself."

"Was she still in bed then?"

"I didn't look."

Kaitlyn sighed. All right, then, forget about Lydia, she told herself. There's nothing you can do. "Actually, I came out here to talk about *you,*" she said to Gabriel.

Gabriel gave her a searing glance. All he said was "No."

"Gabriel—"

"It can't go on, Kaitlyn. Don't you see that? Why can't you just leave me to deal with things my way?"

"Because your way means people get hurt!"

He froze. Then he said distinctly, "So does yours."

Kaitlyn didn't understand—she wasn't sure she *wanted* to understand. Gabriel seemed . . . vulnerable . . . just now. She slapped down the strange, impossible thought that sprang to mind and said, "If you mean me, I can handle myself. If you mean Rob . . ."

The vulnerability disappeared instantly. Gabriel straightened and gave one of his most disturbing smiles.

"Let's say I meant Rob," he said. "What's he going to do when he finds out?"

"He'll understand. I wish you'd let me *tell* him. He might be able to help."

Gabriel's smile just grew more unpleasant. "You think so?"

"I'm *positive*. Rob likes to help people. And, believe it or not, I think he likes *you*. If you weren't so touchy—"

Gabriel waved a hand in sharp dismissal. "I don't want to talk about him."

"Fine. Let's talk about what you're going to do tonight. Going hunting? Going to find some girl walking alone and grab her?" Kaitlyn stepped closer as she spoke. Dim as it was, she could see the immediate wariness on Gabriel's face.

That's it, she thought. All I have to do is get near enough. His control is so close to breaking . . .

Gabriel didn't say anything, so she went on. "Whoever she is, she won't know what you're doing. She'll fight you, and that will hurt her. And she probably won't have enough energy, so you'll probably kill her. . . ."

Kaitlyn was very near now. She could see Gabriel's eyes, see the tortured struggle there. She could feel just the flash of his thought, quickly muffled. *Danger.* Quietly she said, "Is that what you want to happen?"

A muscle in his jaw jerked. "You know it isn't," he raged, equally quiet. "But there isn't any other choice—"

"Oh, Gabriel, don't be *stupid,*" Kaitlyn said and put her arms around him.

He managed to resist for about one and a half seconds.

Then, with shaking hands, he pushed her hair off

her neck. His lips were so near the place already. Kaitlyn bent her head to make it easy for him.

A feeling of something blowing open, breaking through . . . and then something being released. Something like an electric current or a streak of lightning. Kaitlyn relaxed, giving willingly.

And felt her emotions rising to the surface, like blood rising to the surface of heated skin. Her caring for Gabriel, her longing to help him. She could sense his feelings, too.

It was only then that she realized, that she remembered, what the true danger in this was. Only then that she understood what Gabriel had meant by his warnings.

Because she could *feel* what he felt. And along with the gratitude, the sheer satisfaction and relief, were other emotions. Appreciation, joy, wonder, and—oh, dear God, *love.* . . .

Gabriel loved her.

She could see herself in his mind, an image so cloaked in glamour and ethereal grace that she could scarcely recognize it. A girl with red-gold hair like a meteor trail and smoky-blue eyes with strange rings in them. An exotic creature that burned like an eager flame. More witch than human.

How could she have been so *stupid?*

But it had never occurred to her that Gabriel, prickly, untouchable Gabriel, could fall in love with anyone. He'd changed too much since he'd loved Iris—and killed her. He'd become too hard, too bitter.

Only he hadn't.

There was no possibility of misunderstanding.

Kaitlyn could feel his emotions clearly—she was surrounded by them, immersed in them. After two days of deprivation Gabriel's control had splintered and his barriers dissolved completely. He realized what she was seeing, but he couldn't stop her, because he was too desperate in his feeding to fight.

Kait had the sense that they were staring at each other across a narrow chasm, both frozen in place, unable to hide from the other. She was seeing into Gabriel's naked soul. And that wasn't right, that wasn't fair, because she knew what he'd be seeing in her. Friendship and concern, that was all. She couldn't love Gabriel; she was already in love. . . .

But with Gabriel's emotions swirling around her, crashing around both of them like a storm-swelled wave, it was hard to remember that. It was hard to keep any rational thought in mind. Gabriel's love was pulling at her, dragging at her, demanding that she return it. That she give herself completely, open and give him everything. . . .

What are you doing to her?

Kaitlyn's heart stopped.

It was Rob's voice, and it shattered her world like a bolt of lightning. In one instant the sea-swept warmth of Gabriel's passion disappeared. The connection between them was cut off, and they sprang apart . . .

Like guilty lovers, Kaitlyn thought.

Rob was standing just below one of the wrought-iron Victorian streetlights. He was fully dressed, but his hair was still rumpled into a lion's mane from sleep. He looked angry—and bewildered.

And despite his words, he hadn't grabbed Gabriel or tried to pull them apart. Which meant he knew. He must have sensed in the web that Kait wasn't being attacked.

There was a long moment when all three of them just stood. Like statues, Kaitlyn thought wildly. Pillars of salt. She knew that every second she delayed explaining made the thing look worse. But she still couldn't believe it was happening.

Gabriel seemed to be in shock, too. He stood as paralyzed as Kait, his gray eyes dilated.

At last Kait managed to speak through dry lips. "Rob, I was going to tell you—"

It was a terrible choice of words. Rob's face drained of color, and his golden eyes went so dark they were lightless.

"You don't need to," he said. "I saw." He swallowed and then said in an odd, husky voice, "I understand."

Then he turned quickly, almost running. Running away.

Rob, no! That's not what I meant! Rob, wait—

But Rob was almost at the concrete stairs leading to the harbor street. Hurrying to get out of range.

Kaitlyn cast one wild look after him. Then she looked at Gabriel, who was still standing motionless in the shadows. His face revealed nothing, but Kaitlyn could feel his pain.

Her heart was pounding madly. They both needed her, and she could only help one of them. There was no more than a moment to choose.

With an agonized look at Gabriel, she whirled and ran after Rob.

* * *

She caught Rob beneath another streetlight, one with hanging baskets of flowers suspended from a crosspiece.

"Rob, please—you have to *listen* to me. You—"

She was almost hysterical, unable to finish her sentence. He turned, his eyes the wide hurt eyes of a child.

"It's all right," he said. With a jolt Kaitlyn realized something else. Those eyes were *blind*—he wasn't really seeing her. And he certainly wasn't listening.

"Rob, it's not what you think." The dreadful cliché rolled off her tongue before she could stop it. Then she said, with ferocious intensity, "It *isn't*. Aren't you even going to give me a chance to explain?"

That got through. Rob winced and recoiled just a bit, as if he'd rather run away again. But he said, "Of course you can explain."

She could see him bracing himself, waiting for an explanation of why she wanted to leave him. Frustration crested in her, overriding her fear. Words came out in a breathless rush.

"Gabriel and I weren't—we weren't doing anything wrong. I was giving him *energy*, Rob—like you do when you're healing. The crystal did something awful to him, and now he needs life energy every day. He's been in hell this last week. And if I don't help him, he'll hunt somebody down on the streets, and maybe kill them."

Rob blinked. He still looked like some tousled kid who'd been dealt a mortal blow, but now doubt was creeping into his expression. He repeated slowly, "The crystal?"

"I think that's what did it. He was never like this before. Now he needs the energy to stay alive. Rob, you *have* to believe me."

"But—why didn't you tell me?" Rob was shaking his head now, as if he had water in his ear. He looked dazed.

"I wanted to tell you, I did, but he wouldn't let me." And now I've betrayed his confidence, Kaitlyn thought. But there had been nothing else to do. She had to make Rob understand. "And no wonder he wouldn't, after the way you guys all talked about psychic vampires. He knew you'd be disgusted, and he couldn't stand that. So he kept it a secret."

Rob was wavering. Kait could see that he wanted to believe her, and that he was having trouble. Struggling for a leap of faith.

A voice behind Kaitlyn said, "It's all true."

13

Kaitlyn whirled to see the most unlikely person imaginable. Lydia. Looking fragile and wistful, her blue-black hair a liquidy mass under the streetlight's soft illumination.

"You!" Kaitlyn said. "Where have you been? Why did you leave the room?"

Lydia hesitated, then shrugged. "I saw Gabriel leave. I wondered where he was going in the middle of the night, so I followed him to the wharf. And then I saw you come—"

"You spied on us!" It must have been Lydia she'd heard going out the door, Kaitlyn realized. Gabriel had already left.

"Yes," Lydia said, half miserably, half defiantly. "I spied on you. But it's a good thing I did!" She looked at Rob. "Kaitlyn kept saying she wanted to tell you. And she was only doing it because otherwise Gabriel would hurt people, maybe kill them. I don't understand exactly what it's all about, but I know she wasn't messing around with him."

Rob's whole body had relaxed—uncrumpling, Kaitlyn thought. And her own heartbeat was easing. Some of the nightmare feeling of unreality was fading away.

She looked at Rob and he looked at her. For a moment even communication in the web was unnecessary. Kait could see his love, and his longing.

Then, without quite knowing how she'd gotten there, she was in his arms.

"I'm sorry," Rob whispered. And then: *I'm so sorry, Kait. I thought . . . But I could understand why you might want to be with him. You're the only one he cares about. . . .*

It's my fault, Kaitlyn thought back, clinging to him as if she could make them into one body, fuse them together permanently. *I should have told you before, and I'm sorry. But—*

But we won't talk about it any more, Rob said, holding her more tightly. *We'll forget it ever happened.*

Yes. In that moment it seemed to Kaitlyn that she *could* forget. "But we have to make sure Gabriel's all right," she said aloud. "I left him by the wharf. . . ."

Slowly and reluctantly Rob let go of her. "We'll go now," he said. His face still bore the marks of recent emotion; there were shadows under his eyes and his mouth was not quite steady. But Kaitlyn could feel the quiet purpose in him. He wanted to help. "I'll explain to him that I didn't understand. All that talk about psychic vampires—I didn't know."

"I'll go, too," Lydia said. She had been watching

them with open curiosity. For once, Kaitlyn didn't mind, and she gave Lydia a look of gratitude as they started walking. The girl might be nosy, she might be sneaky, and she might have a father who belonged in a horror movie—but she'd done Kaitlyn a good turn tonight. Kaitlyn wouldn't forget that.

Gabriel wasn't at the wharf.

"Hunting?" Rob said, looking at Kait with concern.

"I don't think so. He took enough from me—" Kaitlyn broke off as Rob's arm around her tightened. Rob was shaking his head.

"He can't do that anymore," he muttered. "It could hurt you. We'll have to figure something out. . . ." He shook his head again, preoccupied.

Kaitlyn said nothing. Her happiness was dimming a bit. She was all right with Rob again—but Gabriel was in bad trouble, worse even than Rob knew. She couldn't tell Rob what she'd seen in Gabriel's mind.

But she was dead certain Gabriel wasn't going to accept help from Rob—or from her, ever again.

The next morning Gabriel was back. Kaitlyn was surprised. She and Rob had returned to the hotel the night before to find Anna and Lewis still sitting up. Rob had awakened them both when he found Kait, Gabriel, and Lydia missing.

At Rob's insistence Kait had explained as best she could about Gabriel's condition. Anna and Lewis had been shocked and sorry—and had promised to do anything they could to help.

But Gabriel didn't want help. The next morning he wouldn't talk to anyone and would barely glance at

Kait. There was a strange, glittering look in his eyes, and all Kait could sense from him was determination.

He's hoping that the people in the white house can help him, she guessed. And other than that, he doesn't care about anything.

"We're in deep trouble financially," Anna was saying. "There's enough for gas and breakfast, maybe lunch, and then . . ."

"We'll just have to find the place today," Rob said, with typical Rob-ish optimism. But Kaitlyn knew what he left unspoken. They found the place today or they had to quit, resort to robbery, or use Lydia's credit cards and risk being traced.

"Let's go over what we're looking for," she said. What she really meant was that it was time to tell Lydia. *I think we can trust her,* she added, and Rob nodded. Lewis, of course, agreed wholeheartedly. Kaitlyn was getting a little worried about him—it was clear that he was more than infatuated with Lydia, but Lydia seemed to be the type to play the field.

Gabriel was the only one who might have objected, and he was sitting by the window, ignoring them all.

"A little peninsula thing with rocks on it," Lewis said promptly with a grin at Lydia.

"With *inuk shuk,*" Anna said. "Lining both sides. And the shore behind it is rocky, and behind that is a bank with trees. Spruce and fir, I think. And maybe some scotch broom."

"And the ocean is cold and clean and the waves only come from the right," Kaitlyn put in.

"And it's called something like Griffin's Pit," Rob finished and smiled at her. There was still something of apology, of regret, about his slow smile this morning. Kait felt a twinge in her chest.

"Or Whiff and Spit or Wyvern's Bit," she said lightly, smiling back. Then she said, turning back toward Lydia, "And across from it is a cliff—although heaven knows how that can be, unless it's another little island. And on the cliff is a white house, and that's where we're going."

Lydia nodded. She wasn't stupid; she'd taken all of this in. Her eyes said "thank you" to Kait. "So where do we search today?"

"Flip a coin again," Lewis began, but Rob said, "Let Kaitlyn decide." When Kait looked at him, he added seriously, "Sometimes you have intuitions. And I trust . . . your instinct."

Kaitlyn's eyes stung. She understood; he trusted *her*.

"Let's go the other way today, west. The water didn't feel quite right yesterday. Not . . . enclosed . . . enough." She herself wasn't sure what she meant by that, but everyone else nodded, accepting it.

They skipped breakfast and started driving northwest.

The weather was lovely for a change, and Kaitlyn found herself pathetically grateful for sunshine. Huge puffy white clouds drifted overhead. The coastal road quickly narrowed to one lane and trees crowded around them.

"It's the rain forest," Anna said. To Kaitlyn it was an almost frightening display of plant life. The road seemed to cut through a *solid* swath of vegetation. It was like a puzzle shaped like a wall on either side of the road—the pieces were different colors for different plants, but they interlocked solidly to fill all the space between the ground and the sky.

"We can't even *see* the ocean," Lewis said. "How're we supposed to tell if we're near the place?"

He was right. Kaitlyn groaned inwardly; maybe west had been a bad idea after all. Rob just said, "We'll have to go down side roads every so often and check. And we'll ask people again."

The problem was that there were few side roads and fewer people to ask. The road simply went on and on, winding through the forest, allowing them only occasional glimpses of the coast.

Kaitlyn tried not to feel discouraged, but as they drove farther and farther, her head began to buzz and the emptiness in her middle to expand. She felt as if they'd been driving forever, through three states and a foreign country. And they were never going to find the white house—in fact, the white house probably didn't exist. . . .

"Hey," Lewis said. "Food."

It was another of the kiosks, like the ones that had sold daffodils in Oregon. But this sign said BREAD DAYS: FRIDAY, SATURDAY, SUNDAY.

"It's Sunday," Lewis said. "And I'm starving."

They took two loaves of multigrain bread—and paid for them, because Rob insisted. Kaitlyn hadn't realized how hungry she was until she took the first bite. The bread was dense and moist, cool from the cold air outside. It had a nutty, nourishing flavor, and Kait felt strength and optimism flowing back through her.

"Let's stop *there,*" she said as they passed a small building. A sign proclaimed it to be the SOOKE MUSEUM. She didn't have much hope, first of all because the big museum in Victoria hadn't helped them, and second because this place looked closed, but she was in the mood to try anything.

It *was* closed, but a woman finally answered Rob's persistent knocking. There were piles of books on the floor inside, and a man with a pencil behind his ear, taking inventory.

"I'm sorry," the woman began, but Rob was already talking.

"We don't want to bother you, ma'am," he said, turning the southern charm on full force. "We just have one question—we're looking for a place that might be around here, and we thought you could maybe help us find it."

"What place?" the woman said with a harassed glance behind her, obviously impatient to get back to her work.

"Well, we don't exactly know the name. But it's like a little peninsula, and it's got these rock towers all up and down it."

Kaitlyn held up her drawing of the *inuk shuk.* Please, she was thinking. Oh, please . . .

The woman shook her head. Her look said she thought Kaitlyn and Rob were crazy. "No, I don't know where you'd find anything like that."

Kaitlyn's shoulders sagged. She and Rob glanced at each other in defeat. "Thank you," Rob said dully.

They both turned away and were actually leaving when the man inside the museum spoke up.

"Aren't there some of those things out at Whiffen Spit?"

Every cell in Kaitlyn's body turned into ice.

Whiffen Spit. Whiffen Spit, Whiffenspit, *Whiffen-spit* . . . It was as if the whispering chorus of voices was once again in her mind.

Rob, fortunately, seemed able to move. He spun and got a foot in the door the woman was closing.

"What did you say?"

"Out at Whiffen Spit. I've got a map here some-where. I don't know what the rocks are for, but they've been there as long as I can remember. . . ."

He went on talking, but Kait couldn't hear him over the roaring in her own ears. She wanted to scream, to run around crazily, to turn cartwheels. Anna and Lewis were clutching each other, laughing and gasping, trying to maintain their composure in front of the museum people. The whole web was vibrating with pure joy.

We found it! We found it! Kaitlyn told them. She had to tell someone.

Yeah, and it's Whiffenspit, Lewis said, running it together into one word as Kaitlyn had. *Not Griffin's Pit or Whippin' Bit—*

Rob was closest, Anna said. *Whiff and Spit was actually pretty good.*

Kaitlyn looked toward the car, where Lydia and Gabriel were standing as if declaring themselves both outsiders. Lydia was wide-eyed, watching with inter-est. Gabriel—

Gabriel, aren't you happy? Kaitlyn asked.

I'll be happy when I see it.

"Well, you're *going* to see it, ol' buddy," Rob said, turning and calling with a reckless disregard for the museum people. "I've got a map here!" He waved it triumphantly, his grin nearly splitting his face.

"Well, don't just stand around talking!" Kait said. "Let's go!"

They left the museum people staring after them.

"I can't believe it's real," Kaitlyn kept whispering as they drove.

"Look at this," Lewis was saying excitedly over her. "This map shows why there are only waves coming from the right. It's in the mouth of a little bay, and on the right side is the ocean. The other side is Sooke Basin, and there wouldn't be any waves there."

Rob turned on a narrow side road, nearly invisible between the trees. When he parked at the end, Kaitlyn was almost afraid to get out.

"Come on," Rob said, extending his hand. "We'll see it together."

Slowly, as if under a spell, Kaitlyn walked with him to the edge of the trees and looked down.

Then her throat swelled and she just stared.

It was the place. It looked exactly as it had in her dreams, a little spit of land pointing like a crooked finger into the water. It was lined with the same boulders, many with *inuk shuk* piled on top of them.

They walked down the rocky beach and onto Whiffen Spit.

Gravel crunched under Kaitlyn's feet. Gulls wheeled in the air, crying. It was all so *familiar. . . .*

"Don't," Rob whispered. "Oh, Kait." It was then that she realized she was crying.

"I'm just happy," she said. "Look." She pointed across the water. Far away, on a distant cliff covered with trees so green they were black, was a single white house.

"It's real," Rob said, and Kait knew he was feeling what she was. "It's really there."

Anna was kneeling by the edge of the spit, moving rocks. "Lewis, get that big one."

Lewis was showing Lydia around. "What are you doing?"

"Building an *inuk shuk.* I don't know why, but I think we should."

"Let's make it a good one," Rob said. He took hold of a large, flat rock, tried to lift it. "Kait—"

He didn't finish. Gabriel had taken hold of the other side.

The two of them looked at each other for a moment. Then Gabriel smiled, a thin smile touched with bitterness, but not with hatred.

Rob returned it with his own smile. Not as bright as usual, with something like apology behind it, and hope for the future.

Together, they lifted the stone and hauled it to Anna.

Everyone helped build the *inuk shuk.* It was a good big one, and sturdy. When they were done, Kait wiped wet dirt off her hands.

"Now it's time to find the white house," she said.

From the map they could see why there was land across the water. It was the other side of the mouth of Sooke Basin. They would have to drive back the way they'd come, and then all the way around the basin— or as far as the side roads would take them.

They drove for well over an hour, and then the road ran out.

"We'll have to walk from here," Rob said, looking into the dense mass of rain forest ahead.

"Let's just hope we don't get lost," Kait muttered.

It was cool and icy fresh in the forest. It smelled like Christmas trees and cedar and wetness. With every step Kaitlyn could hear her own feet squishing in the undergrowth and feel herself sinking—as if she were walking on cushions.

"It's sort of primeval, isn't it?" Lydia gasped, picking her way around a fallen log. "Makes you think of dinosaurs."

Kaitlyn knew what she meant. It was a place where people didn't belong, where the plant kingdom ruled. All around her things were growing on other things: ferns on trees, little seedlings on stumps, moss on everything.

"Did anybody ever see the movie *Babes in Toyland?*" Lewis asked in a muted voice. "Remember the Forest of No Return?"

They walked for several hours before they were certain they were lost.

"The problem is that we can't see the sun!" Rob said in exasperation. The sky had gone gray again, and between the clouds and the canopy of green above them, they had no way to get their bearings.

"The problem is that we shouldn't have just barged in here in the first place," Gabriel snapped back.

"How else are we supposed to get to the white house?"

"I don't know, but this is stupid."

Another argument, shaping up to be a classic.

171

Kaitlyn turned away, to find Anna staring fixedly at something on a branch. A bird, Kaitlyn saw, blue with a high pointed crest.

"What is it?"

Anna answered without looking at her. "A Steller's jay."

"Oh. Is it rare?"

"No, but it's smart," Anna murmured. "Smart enough to recognize a clearing with a house. And it can get above the trees."

Understanding crashed in on Kaitlyn, and she had to suppress a whoop. She said in a choked voice, "You mean—"

"Yes. Hush." Anna went on staring at the bird. In the web, power thrummed around her, rose from her like waves of heat. The jay made a harsh noise like *shaaaack* and fluttered its wings.

Rob and Gabriel stopped arguing and turned to goggle.

"What's she *doing?*" Lydia hissed. Kait shushed her, but Anna answered.

"Seeing through its eyes," she murmured. "Giving it my vision—a white house." She continued to stare at the bird, her face rapt, her body swaying just slightly. Her fathomless owl's eyes were mystical, her long dark hair moved with her swaying.

She looks like a shaman, Kaitlyn thought. Some ancient priestess communing with nature, becoming part of it. Anna was the only one of them who really seemed to belong in the forest.

"It knows what to look for," Anna said at last. "Now—"

With a rapid-fire burst of noise like *shook, shook, shook,* the jay took off. It went straight up, into the canopy of branches—and disappeared.

"I know where it is," Anna said, her face still intent and trancelike. "Come on!"

They followed her, scrambling over mossy logs, splashing through shallow streams. It was rough going over steep ground, and Anna always seemed to be just on the verge of vanishing into the trees. They kept following until the light began to dim and Kaitlyn was ready to drop.

"We've got to take a rest," she gasped, stopping by a stream where huge fleshy yellow flowers grew.

"We can't stop now," Anna called back. "We're there."

Kaitlyn jumped up, feeling as if she could run a marathon. "Are you sure? Can you see it?"

"Come here," Anna said, standing with one hand on a moss-bedecked cedar. Kaitlyn looked over her shoulder.

"Oh . . ." she whispered.

The white house stood on a little knoll in a clearing. This close Kaitlyn could see it was not alone. There were several outbuildings around it, weathered and splintery. The house itself was bigger than Kaitlyn had thought.

"We made it," Rob whispered, behind her. Kaitlyn leaned against him, too full of emotion to speak, even in the web.

When they'd found Whiffen Spit, she'd felt like singing and shouting. They had all been rowdy in celebration. But, here, shouting would have been

173

wrong. This was a deeper happiness, mixed with something like reverence. For a long while they all just stood and looked at the house from their visions.

Then a harsh, drawn-out *shaaaak* broke into their reverie. The jay was fluttering on a branch, scolding them.

Anna laughed and looked at it, and it swooped away. "I told it thank you," she said. "And that it could leave. So now we'd better go forward, because we'll never find our way back."

Kaitlyn felt awkward and self-conscious as she walked out of the shelter of the trees, down toward the house. What if they don't want us here? she thought helplessly. What if it's all a mistake . . . ?

"Do you see any people?" Lewis whispered as they came abreast of the first outbuilding.

"No," Kaitlyn began, and then she did.

The building was a barn, and there was a woman inside. She was forking hay and dung, handling the big pitchfork very capably for someone as small and light as she was. When she saw Kaitlyn she stopped and looked without saying a word.

Kaitlyn stared at her, drymouthed. Then Rob spoke up.

"We're here," he said simply.

The woman was still looking at each of them. She was tiny and elegant, and Kait couldn't tell if she were Egyptian or Asian. Her eyes were tilted but blue, her skin was the color of coffee with cream. Her black hair was done in some complicated fashion, with silver ornaments.

Suddenly she smiled.

"Of course!" she said. "We've been expecting you. But I thought there were only five."

"We, uh, sort of picked up Lydia on the way," Rob said. "She's our friend, and we can vouch for her. But you do know us, ma'am?"

"Of course, of course!" She had an almost indefinable accent—not like the Canadians Kaitlyn had heard. "You're the children we've been calling to. And I'm Mereniang. Meren if that's too long. And you must come inside and meet the others."

Relief sifted through Kaitlyn. Everything was going to be all right. Their search was over.

"Yes, you must all come inside," Mereniang was saying, dusting off her hands. Then she looked at Gabriel. "Except him."

14

W hat?" Kaitlyn said, and Rob said, "What do you mean, except him?"

Mereniang turned. Her face was still pleasant, but Kait suddenly realized it was also remote. And her eyes . . .

Kaitlyn had seen eyes like that only once before, when the man with the caramel-colored skin had stopped her in the airport. When she'd looked into his eyes, she'd had the sense of centuries passing. Millennia. So many years that the very attempt to comprehend them sent her reeling.

There were ice ages in this woman's eyes, too.

Kaitlyn heard her own gasp. "Who *are* you?" she blurted before she could stop herself.

The enigmatic blue eyes dropped, veiled by heavy lashes. "I told you. Mereniang." Then the eyes lifted again, held steady. "One of the Fellowship," the woman said. "And we don't have many rules here, but this one can't be broken. No one may come into the house who has taken a human life."

She looked at Gabriel and added, "I'm sorry."

A wave of pure fury swept over Kait. She could feel herself flushing. But Rob spoke before she could, and he was as angry as she'd ever seen him.

"You can't do that!" he said. "Gabriel hasn't— what if it was self-defense?" he demanded incoherently.

"I'm sorry," Mereniang said again. "I can't change the rules. Aspect forbids it." She seemed regretful but composed, perfectly willing to stand here all evening and debate the issue. Relaxed but unbending, Kait thought dazedly. Absolutely unbending.

"Who's Aspect?" Lewis demanded.

"Not who. What. Aspect is our philosophy, and it doesn't make exceptions for accidental killing."

"But you can't just shut him out," Rob stormed. "You *can't.*"

"He'll be taken care of. There's a cabin beyond the gardens where he can stay. It's just that he can't enter the house."

The web was singing with outrage. Rob said flatly, "Then we can't enter it, either. We're not going without him!"

There was absolute conviction in his voice. And it rallied Kaitlyn out of her speechless daze. "He's right," she said. "We're not."

"He's one of us," Anna said.

"And it's a stupid rule!" Lewis added.

They were all standing shoulder to shoulder, united in their determination. All but Lydia, who stood aside looking uncertain—and Gabriel.

Gabriel had moved back, away from them. He was wearing the thin, faint smile he'd given Rob earlier.

"Go on," he said directly to Rob. "You have to."

"No, we don't." Rob was right in front of him now. Golden in the blue twilight, contrasting with Gabriel's pale face and dark hair. Sun and black hole, Kaitlyn thought. Eternal opposites. Only this time they were fighting *for* each other.

"Yes, you do," Gabriel said. "Go in there and find out what's going on. I'll wait. I don't care."

A lie Kait could feel clearly in the web. But no one mentioned it. Mereniang was still waiting with the patience of someone to whom minutes were nothing.

Slowly Rob let out his breath. "All right," he said at last. His voice was grim and the look he turned on Mereniang not friendly.

"Wait here," Mereniang told Gabriel. "Someone will come for you." She began walking toward the house.

Kaitlyn followed, but her legs felt heavy and she looked back twice. Gabriel looked almost small standing there by himself in the gathering darkness.

The white house was made of stone, and spacious inside, with a cathedral hush about it. The floor was stone, too. It might have been a temple.

But the furniture, what Kaitlyn could see of it, was simple. There were carved wooden benches and chairs that looked Colonial. She glimpsed a loom in one of the many recessed chambers.

"How old is this place?" she asked Mereniang.

"Old. And it's built on the remnants of an older house. But we'll talk about that later. Right now you're all tired and hungry—come in here and I'll bring you something to eat."

She ushered them into a room with an enormous fireplace and a long cedar table. Kaitlyn sat on a bench, feeling flustered, resentful, and *wrong.*

She went on feeling it as Mereniang returned, balancing a heavy wooden tray. A young girl was behind her, also carrying a tray.

"Tamsin," Mereniang introduced her. The girl was very pretty, with clusters of curly yellow hair and the profile of a Grecian maiden. Like Mereniang and the man at the airport, she seemed to have the characteristics of several different races, harmoniously blended.

But they're not what I expected, Kaitlyn told Rob wretchedly.

It wasn't that they weren't magical enough. They were almost *too* magical, despite their simple furniture and ordinary ways. There was something alien at the core of them, something disturbing about the way they stood and watched. Even the young girl, Tamsin, seemed older than the giant trees outside.

The food was good, though. Bread like the loaves they'd bought at the kiosk, fresh and nutty. Some soft, pale yellow cheese. A salad that seemed to be made of more wild plants than lettuce—flowers and what looked like weeds. But delicious. Some flat purply-brown things that looked like fruit roll-ups.

"They *are* fruit roll-ups," Anna said when Lewis asked. "They're made of salal berries and salmonberries."

There was no meat, not even fish.

"If you're finished, you can come meet the others," Mereniang said.

Kaitlyn bridled slightly. "What about Gabriel?"

"I've had someone take food to him."

"No, I mean, doesn't *he* get to meet the others? Or do you have a rule against that, too?"

Mereniang sighed. She clasped her small, square-fingered hands together. Then she put them on her hips.

"I'll do what I can," she said. "Tamsin, take them out to the rose garden. It's the only place warm enough. I'll be along."

The rose garden's warm? Lewis asked as they followed Tamsin outside.

Strangely enough, it was. There were roses blooming, too, all colors, crimson and golden-orange and blush pink. The light and warmth seemed to come from the fountain in the center of the walled garden.

No, not the fountain, Kaitlyn thought. The crystal in the fountain. When she'd first seen it in a picture, she hadn't known what it was; she'd wondered if it was an ice sculpture or a column.

It wasn't like Mr. Z's crystal. That monstrosity had been covered with obscene growths, smaller crystals that sprouted like parasites from the main body. This crystal was clean and pure, all straight lines and perfect facets.

And it was glowing gently. Pulsing with a soft, milky light that warmed the air around it.

"Energy," Rob said, holding a hand up to feel it. "It's got a bioenergetic field."

Kaitlyn felt a ripple in the web and was turning even as Gabriel said, "Beats a campfire."

"You're here!" Rob said. They all gathered around him happily. Even Lydia was smiling.

At the same moment Mereniang came through the other entrance in the wall with a group of people.

"This is Timon," she said. The man who stepped forward actually looked old. He was tall but frail and white-haired. His lined face was gentle, the skin almost transparent.

Is he the leader? Kaitlyn asked silently.

"I am a poet and historian," Timon said. "But as the oldest member of the colony, I am sometimes forced to make decisions." He gave a gently ironic smile.

Kaitlyn stared at him, her heartbeat quickening. Had he *heard* that?

"And this is LeShan."

"We've already met," Gabriel said and showed his teeth.

It was the caramel-skinned man from the airport. His hair was a pale shimmery brown, like silver birch. His eyes were slanting and very dark, and they flashed at Gabriel dangerously.

"I remember," he said. "The last time I saw you, you had a knife at my throat."

"And you were on top of Kaitlyn," Gabriel said, causing some consternation among the rest of the Fellowship.

"I was trying to warn you!" LeShan snapped, moving forward.

Mereniang was frowning. "LeShan," she said. LeShan went on glaring. "LeShan, Aspect!"

LeShan subsided, stepping back.

If Aspect was a nonviolent philosophy, Kait had the

feeling that LeShan had a little trouble with it. She remembered that he'd had a temper.

"Now," Timon said. "Sit down if you'd like. We'll try to answer your questions."

Kaitlyn sat on one of the cool stone benches that lined the wall. She had so many questions she didn't know which to ask first. In the silence she could hear the singing of frogs and the gentle trickle of water in the fountain. The air was heady with the scent of roses. The pale, milky light of the crystal gave a gentle radiance to Timon's thin hair and Mereniang's lovely face.

No one else was speaking. Lewis nudged her. *Go on.*

"Who are you people?" Kait asked finally.

Timon smiled. "The last survivors of an ancient race. The people of the crystal."

"That's what I heard," Lydia said. "I've heard people use that name, but I don't know what it *means.*"

"Our civilization used crystals for generating and focusing energy. Not just any crystals—they had to be perfectly pure and faceted in a certain way. We called them great crystals or firestones. They were used as power stations; we extracted energy from them the way you extract the energy of heat from coal."

"Is that possible?" Rob said.

"For us it was. But we were a nation of psychics; our society was based on psychic power." Timon nodded toward the crystal in the fountain. *"That* is the last perfect crystal, and we use it to generate the energy to sustain this place. Without it, we would be helpless. You see, the crystals do more than just supply technical power. They sustain *us*. In the old country they could rejuvenate us; here they merely stop the ravages of time."

Is that why so many of them have young faces and old eyes? Kaitlyn wondered. But Lewis was speaking up.

"There's nothing like that in history books," he said. "Nothing about a country that used crystals for power."

"I'm afraid it was before what you consider history," Timon said. "I promise you, the civilization did exist. Plato spoke of it, although he was only repeating stories *he'd* heard. A land where the fairest and noblest race of people lived. Their country was formed of alternating rings of land and water, and their city was surrounded by three walls. They dug up a metal called *orichalcum*, which was as precious as gold and shone with a red light, and they used it to decorate the inner wall."

Kaitlyn was gasping. For as Timon spoke, she *saw* what he described. Images were flooding into her mind, as they had when Joyce had pressed a tiny shard of crystal to her third eye. She saw a city with three circular walls, one of brass, one of tin, and one which glowed red-gold. The city itself was barbaric in its splendor—buildings were coated with silver, their pinnacles with gold.

"They had everything," Timon said in his gentle voice. "Plants of every type; herb, root, and leaf. Hot springs and mineral baths. Excellent soil for growing things. Aqueducts, gardens, temples, docks, libraries, places of learning."

Kaitlyn saw it all. Groves of beautiful trees intermingled with the beautiful buildings. And people living among them without racial strife, in harmony.

"But what *happened?*" she said. "Where did it all go?"

LeShan answered. "They lost respect for the earth. They took and took, without giving anything back."

"They destroyed the environment?" Anna asked.

"It wasn't quite as simple as that," Timon said softly. "In the final days there was a rift between the people who used their powers for good and those who had chosen the service of evil. You see, the crystals could just as easily work evil as good, they could be turned to torture and destruction. A number of people joined the Dark Lodge and began to use them this way."

"And meanwhile the 'good' psychic masters were demanding too much of their own crystals," LeShan put in. "They were greedy. When the energy broadcast from the crystals was tuned too high, it caused an artificial imbalance. It caused earthquakes first, then floods."

"And so the land was destroyed," Timon said sadly. "Most of the people died with it. But a few clairvoyants escaped—they'd been able to predict what was going to happen. Some of them went to Egypt, some to Peru. And some"—he lifted his head and looked at Kait's group—"to Northern America."

Kaitlyn narrowed her eyes. There had been no pictures in her head to accompany Timon's last words. "This—destruction," she said. "It wouldn't have involved a continent sinking or anything, would it? Like a lost continent?"

Timon just smiled. "Ours is certainly a lost race," he said, then went on without answering the question. "This little enclave is all that remains of our people. We came here a long time ago, with the hope of living simply, in peace. We don't bother the outside world, and most of the time it doesn't bother us."

Kaitlyn wanted to pursue her question, but Rob was asking another one. "But, you know, Mr. Zetes—the man we ran away from—he has a crystal, too."

Members of the Fellowship were nodding grimly. "We're the only pure survivors," Mereniang said. "But others escaped and intermarried with the natives of their new lands. Your Mr. Zetes is a descendent of one of those people. He must have inherited that crystal—or possibly unearthed it after it had been hidden for centuries."

"It *looks* different from yours," Rob said. "It's all covered with things like spikes."

"It's evil," Mereniang said simply, her ageless blue eyes clear and sad.

"Well, it did something to Gabriel," Rob said. In the web Kaitlyn could feel Gabriel tense in anticipation. Although he was keeping himself under tight control, she could tell he was both hopeful and resentful. And that he was beginning to suffer as he did every night—he needed energy, soon.

"Mr. Z hooked Gabriel up to it," Rob was going on. "Like you said, for torture. But afterward—well, it had permanent effects."

Mereniang looked at Gabriel, then moved to look at him more closely. She put a hand on his forehead, over his third eye. Gabriel flinched but didn't step back.

"Now, just let me . . ." Mereniang's sentence trailed off. Her eyes were focused on something invisible, her whole attitude one of listening. Kaitlyn had seen Rob look like that when he was healing.

"I see." Mereniang's face had become very serious. She took her hand away. "The crystal stepped up your metabolism. You burn your own energy now so quickly that you need an outside supply."

The words were dispassionate, but Kait was certain she could detect something less impartial in those ageless blue eyes. A certain fastidious distaste.

Oh, God, no, Kait thought. If Gabriel senses that . . .

"There's one thing that might help," Mereniang said. "Put your hands on the crystal."

Gabriel looked at her sharply. Then, slowly, he turned to the crystal in the center of the garden. His face seemed particularly pale in the cool white light as he approached it. After a brief hesitation, he touched one hand to a milky, pulsating facet.

"Both hands," Mereniang said.

Gabriel put his other hand on the crystal. As soon as it touched, his body jerked as if an electrical current had been sent through it. In the web Kaitlyn felt a flare of power.

She was on her feet in alarm. So was Rob, so were the others. But what she felt in the web now was energy flowing, flowing *into* Gabriel. It was cold, and it elicited none of the wild gratitude and joy she'd felt in Gabriel when he took energy from her—but it was feeding him nevertheless. Sustaining him.

She sat down again. Gabriel took his hands away.

He stood with his head down for a moment, and Kaitlyn could see that he was breathing quickly. Then he turned.

"Am I cured?" he asked, looking straight at Mereniang.

"Oh—no." For the first time the dark woman looked uncomfortable. She couldn't seem to hold Gabriel's eyes. "I'm afraid there *is* no cure, except possibly the destruction of the crystal that made you this way. But any crystal which produces energy can help you—"

Rob interrupted, too overwrought to be polite. "Just a minute. You mean destroying Mr. Zetes's crystal will cure him?"

"Possibly."

"Well, then, what are we waiting for? Let's destroy it!"

Mereniang looked helplessly at Timon. All the members of the Fellowship were looking at one another in the same way.

"It isn't that easy," Timon told Rob gently. "To destroy that crystal, we would first have to destroy *this* crystal. The only way to shatter it would be to unite it with a shard from a crystal that is still pure. Still perfect."

"And this is the last perfect crystal," Mereniang reminded them.

"So—you can't help us," Rob said after a moment.

"Not in that, I'm afraid," Mereniang said quietly. Timon sighed.

Kait was looking at Gabriel. His shoulders had sagged abruptly, as if taking on a heavy weight. His head was slightly bent. In the web all she could feel were the walls he was doggedly building brick by brick. She could only guess what he must be feeling.

She knew what her other mind-mates were feeling, though—alarm. The Fellowship couldn't cure Gabriel's psychic vampirism. Well, then, what about their other problem?

"There's something else we wanted to ask you about," Lewis said nervously. "See, when we were trying to figure out what Mr. Z was up to—well, it's a long story, but we ended up with this telepathic link. All of us, you know. And we can't get rid of it."

"Telepathy is one of the gifts of the old race," Timon said. His old eyes rested on Kait briefly, and he smiled. "The ability to communicate mind to mind is a wonderful thing."

"But we can't *stop,*" Lewis said. "Gabriel got us linked, and now we can't get unlinked."

Timon looked at Gabriel. So did Mereniang and several of the others, as if to say, "You again?" Kaitlyn had the distinct impression that they thought he was a troublemaker. She sensed a flash of anger from Gabriel, quickly stifled.

"Yes, well, I'm afraid there's not much we can do about that, either," Mereniang said. "We can study it, of course, but a five-way link is a stable pattern. Usually it can only be broken by—"

"The death of one of the members," Kaitlyn and Anna said in chorus. They looked at each other in despair.

"Or distance," Timon said. "If you were to put physical distance between the members—that wouldn't break the link, of course, but you wouldn't feel it as much."

Rob was rumpling his already tousled hair. "But, look, the really important thing is Mr. Zetes. We understand if you can't fix Gabriel or break the link—but you *are* going to help us against Mr. Z, aren't you?"

There was one of those dreadful pauses which spoke louder than words.

"We are a peaceful race," Timon said at last, almost apologetically.

"But he's *afraid* of you. He thinks you're the only threat to him." Rob glanced for confirmation at Lydia, who nodded.

"We don't have the power of destruction," Mereniang said. LeShan was grinding one fist into his palm—Kaitlyn sensed that he, at least, wished they did.

Rob was still protesting. "You mean there's nothing you can do to stop him? Do you realize what he's *up* to?"

"We are not warriors," Timon said. "Only the youngest of us can even leave this place and travel in the outside world. The rest are too feeble—too old." He sighed again and rubbed his lined forehead.

"But can't you do something psychically?" Kaitlyn asked. "Mr. Z's been attacking us long distance."

"It would give away our location," LeShan said grimly, and Timon nodded.

"Your Mr. Zetes *does* have the power of destruction. If he discovers this place, he will attack us. We are only safe as long as it remains a secret."

Gabriel lifted his head and spoke for the first time in a long while. "You're awfully trusting of *us,* then."

Timon smiled faintly. "When you first came here, Mereniang looked into your hearts. None of you has come to betray us."

Kaitlyn had been listening with growing frustration. Suddenly she couldn't keep quiet any longer. She found herself standing, words bursting out of her throat.

"You can't help Gabriel and you can't help break the link and you won't help us fight Mr. Zetes—so what did you *bring* us here for?"

There was age-old sadness in Mereniang's eyes. Endless regret, tempered with the serenity of resignation.

"To give you a refuge," the dark woman said. "We want you to stay here. Forever."

15

❧

But what about Gabriel?" Kaitlyn said. It was the first thing she could think of.

"He can stay, too."

"Without going in the *house?*"

Before Mereniang could answer, Rob spoke. "Look, *nobody's* deciding to stay right now. This is something we've got to think over—"

"It's the only place you'll be safe," Mereniang said. "We've had a lot of visitors over the years, but we've asked very few to stay with us. We do it when they have no choice—no other safety."

"Are there any here now?" Kait asked, looking at the Fellowship behind Mereniang.

"The last died a long time ago. But he lived longer than he would have in the outside world—and so will you. You are part of our race, and the crystal will help sustain you."

Lewis was twisting his baseball cap. "What do you mean, 'part of your race'?"

191

Timon spread his hands. "All psychics are descendants of the old race. Somewhere among your ancestors was one of the people of the crystal. The old blood has awakened in you." He looked at each of them earnestly. "My children, you *belong* here."

Kait didn't know what to say. She'd never felt so confused and disoriented in her life. The Fellowship was nothing that she had expected, and the discovery left her numb, in shock. Meanwhile, the web was a jumble of conflicting emotions that made it impossible for her to tell what any particular one of the others was thinking.

It was Rob who saved them, speaking steadily. "We're proud that you think we're good enough to join you, sir," he said to Timon. He'd regained his natural courtesy. "And we'd like to thank you. But this is something we're going to have to talk over a bit. You understand that." It was a statement, but Rob scanned the faces of the Fellowship questioningly.

Mereniang looked vaguely annoyed, but Timon said, "Of course. Of course. You're all tired, and you'll find it easier to think tomorrow. There's no hurry."

Kaitlyn still felt like arguing with somebody—but Timon was right. She was swaying on her feet. Tomorrow they'd all be fresh, and less emotional.

"We'll talk to them again about Mr. Zetes then," Rob whispered to her under cover of the meeting breaking up.

Kaitlyn nodded and glanced around for Gabriel. He was talking to Lydia, but he stopped when he saw her looking.

"Are you going to be all right?" she asked him.

His eyes were opaque—as if they'd filmed over with

gray spiderweb. "Sure," he said. "They've got a little cot for me in the toolshed."

"Oh, Gabriel . . . Maybe we should all stay there with you. Do you want me to ask Meren—"

"No," Gabriel said vehemently. Then he added more smoothly, "Don't worry about me. I'll be fine. Get your sleep."

Walls, walls, walls. Kaitlyn sighed.

Then, oddly, he said: "Good night, Kait."

Kaitlyn blinked. Had he ever said good night to her before? "I—good night, Gabriel."

Then Mereniang gathered them up and took them into the house, leaving Gabriel with a couple of the men.

It was as they were entering the house that Kaitlyn remembered a question she'd forgotten to ask. "Meren, do you know about the *inuk shuk* on Whiffen Spit?"

"Timon knows the most about them."

"Well, I was just wondering why they were there. And if they meant anything."

Timon was smiling reminiscently. "Ancient peoples started the tradition. They came down as traders from the north and left some of their stone language here. They called this a place of good magic, and they built their friendship signs on the spit that points to it."

Timon was still smiling, lost in thought. "That was a very long time ago," he said. "We've watched the world change all around us—but we have remained unchanged."

There was a note of pride in his voice, and a tinge of arrogance in Mereniang's face.

Kait looked at Timon. "Don't you think change is sometimes good?"

Timon came out of his reverie, looking startled. But no one answered her.

Kaitlyn's bedroom was very plain, with a bed built into the wall, a chair, and a washbasin under a mirror. It was the first time she'd slept alone—without the others—in a week. She didn't like it, but she was so tired she fell asleep quickly anyway.

Alone in the tool shed, Gabriel was awake.

So Mereniang had "looked into their hearts," had she? He smiled wryly. What the Fellowship didn't seem to realize was that hearts could change. *He* had changed since he'd come here.

It was a change that had started last night. Last night on the wharf when he'd discovered his feelings for Kaitlyn—and Kaitlyn had made her choice.

It wasn't her fault. Strangely enough, it wasn't Kessler's, either. They belonged together, both honest, both good.

But that didn't mean Gabriel had to stick around and watch it.

And now, tonight, his last hope had disappeared. The people of the crystal couldn't free him. They didn't even *want* to. And he'd seen the disgust and condemnation in their eyes.

Live here? In their outbuildings? Face that condemnation every day? And watch Kessler and Kait romancing each other?

Gabriel's lips drew back from his teeth in a fierce smile. He didn't think so.

I should be grateful to the Fellowship, he thought.

They've shown me what I really am, simply in contrast to what *they* are. Back in the old days I'd have joined the Dark Lodge and hunted these gutless wimps out of existence.

It was a fairly simple equation. He didn't belong with the good guys, the white hats. Therefore, he must belong with the other side.

Not a new revelation, but a rediscovery. Kait had almost made him forget what he really was. She'd almost convinced him that he could live on the light side, that he wasn't a killer by nature. Well, tomorrow she'd see how wrong she'd been.

Gabriel stepped back a little to look at the body on the toolshed floor.

The man's name had been Theo. The Fellowship had sent him to spend the night out here—whether as companion or guard Gabriel didn't know. Now he was in a coma. Not quite dead, but getting there.

Gabriel had mind-linked with him to take knowledge from his brain. Including the knowledge of a secret trail through the otherwise impassable forest.

The extra energy had been nice, too.

Now the only thing Gabriel was waiting for was Lydia. He'd whispered a few words to her in the rose garden, asking her to come tonight and meet him. He was fairly certain she'd show up.

And then Gabriel would ask her if she really wanted to spend the next seventy years with a commune of doddering old hippies. Or if life might not be better back in sunny California, where Gabriel had the feeling that Mr. Zetes was setting up a little Dark Lodge of his own.

Lydia was weak. He thought he could persuade her.

And if he couldn't—well, she could join Theo on the floor. Lewis would be unhappy, but what did Lewis matter?

For just an instant an image flashed through his mind of what would happen if he *could* persuade her. What would happen here, to the Fellowship, once he gave Mr. Zetes the information needed to home in on the white house. It wouldn't be a pretty picture. And Kait would be in the middle of it. . . .

Gabriel shook the thought off and bared his teeth again.

He had to at least have the courage of his convictions. If he was going to be evil, he'd *be* evil, all the way. From now on there were no half measures.

And besides, Kessler would be here. He'd just have to take care of Kaitlyn himself.

A footstep sounded outside the shed. Gabriel turned to meet Lydia, smiling.

Someone was shouting.

Kaitlyn could hear it even in her sleep, as she slowly drifted toward consciousness. By the time she was fully awake, it was more than one person, and the web was singing with alarm.

She ran out, pulling on her clothes. Broadcasting *What's happening?* to anyone that could hear.

I don't know, Rob sent back. *Everyone's upset. Something's happened.* . . .

People were running in the hallways of the white house. Kaitlyn spotted Tamsin and swooped on her.

"What's going *on?*"

"Your friends," Tamsin said. She had olive-dark

eyes, contrasting strangely with her golden hair. "The boy outside and the small girl . . ."

"Gabriel and Lydia? *What?*"

"They're gone," Mereniang said, appearing from a recessed room. "And the man we had guarding Gabriel is nearly dead."

Kaitlyn's heart plummeted. Endlessly, it seemed. She couldn't move or breathe.

It couldn't be true. It *couldn't*. Gabriel wouldn't have done a thing like that. . . .

But then she remembered how he'd looked last night. His gray eyes so opaque, his walls so high. As if he'd lost all hope.

And she certainly couldn't sense him anywhere in the web. She could feel only Rob and Lewis and Anna, who were coming to join her now in the hallway.

Rob put an arm around her to support her. Kaitlyn needed it; she thought her knees might give out.

Lewis was looking wretched and unbelieving. "Lydia went, too?" he asked pathetically. Mereniang just nodded.

"But they can't have gone far," Kait whispered, finding her voice. "They can't get through the forest."

"The guard knew a path. Gabriel entered his mind. He knows what the guard knew." Mereniang spoke with very little emotion.

"It must have been Lydia," Rob exploded. "Gabriel wouldn't have done it on his own. Lydia must have talked him into it, somehow." Kaitlyn could feel his pain and Lewis's fighting each other, building exponentially, magnifying her own distress.

Mereniang shook her head once, decisively. "If

anything, it was the other way around. I realized last night that Gabriel was dangerous; that was why I sent Theo to watch him. But I underestimated *how* dangerous he was."

Kaitlyn felt a wave of sickness. "I still can't believe it. It couldn't have been his fault—"

"And I still don't think it was Lydia's fault," Lewis began.

"It doesn't matter whose fault it is," Mereniang said sharply, interrupting both of them. "And there's no time to argue. We have to prepare for an attack."

Lewis looked confused and horrified. "You're going to attack—?"

"No! We're going to *be* attacked. As soon as those two communicate with your Mr. Zetes. They must have run away to join him."

This time the wave of sickness almost drowned Kaitlyn. She heard Anna whisper, "Oh, no . . ."

And she tried to convince herself that Gabriel wouldn't tell Mr. Zetes, that he'd just run away. But the violent beating of her own heart contradicted her.

"Mereniang! We need you in the garden!" The voice came from a doorway.

Mereniang turned. "I'm coming!" She looked back at Kaitlyn's group. "Stay inside. The worst of it will be out there." And then she was running.

Kaitlyn held on to Rob, her only anchor in a spinning world. *Do you think he'll do it?*

Rob's arms tightened around her. *I don't know.*

Rob, is it our fault?

The hardest question, the one she knew would haunt her dreams if she lived through today. She could feel Lewis's hurt despair. Before Rob could answer, the attack began.

A cold wind blew down the corridor. Not just cold air; a gale. It whipped Kaitlyn's hair against her cheeks and tore loose strands from Anna's braid. It cut through their clothing like a newly sharpened knife.

And with it came a rattling. The wooden bench against the wall began to tremble, at first with a fine vibration, then more and more violently. Kaitlyn could hear the banging of doors swinging on their hinges, and the crash of things falling off shelves and walls.

It was so sudden that for a moment all she could do was stand and cling to Rob. Her temperature seemed to have dropped by degrees. A violent shivering racked her body.

"Stay together," Rob shouted, reaching out for Anna and Lewis. They grabbed hold, all four of them clutching each other. It was like trying to stand in a blizzard.

There was a wild ringing in Kaitlyn's ears—like the sound she'd heard once in the van. The sound of a crystal glass being stroked, only this went on and on, and it was pitched at a frequency that hurt. That pierced like needles, making it almost impossible to think.

And the *smell*. The odor of rotting flesh, of raw sewage. The wind forced it into her nostrils.

"What are they trying to do? Stink us all out?" Lewis shouted.

"Meren said it would be worse outside!" Anna

shouted back. It was no good using telepathy, the entire web was vibrating with that piercing note.

"And they said she was needed in the *garden!*" Rob shouted. "The garden—where the crystal is. Come on!"

"Come on *where?*" Lewis yelled.

"To the rose garden! Maybe we can do something to help!"

They stumbled and staggered getting out of the house. Outside, the wind was worse, and the sky was black with clouds. It didn't seem to be morning at all, but an eerie and unnatural twilight.

"Come on!" Rob kept shouting, and somehow they made it to the garden.

The smell was coming from here, and so was the ringing sound. The roses were tattered, their petals torn off by the wind. A few petals still whirled in the air.

"Oh, God—the crystal!" Anna shouted.

Most of the Fellowship seemed to be gathered around it, and many of them, including Timon and Mereniang, had their hands on it. The crystal itself was pulsating wildly, but not with the gentle milky light Kait had seen before. Every color of the rainbow seemed to be fighting and flashing in its depths. It was dazzling, almost impossible to look at.

But that wasn't what Anna had meant. It was something much worse. Superimposed on the rose garden crystal was another, a phantom crystal without any color. A monstrosity with growths sprouting from every facet.

The crystal from Mr. Z's basement, Kait thought dazedly. Or, rather, its astral image. And around that corrupted crystal were the astral images of the attackers, visible like ghosts among the bodies of the Fellowship.

The gray people, the ones she'd seen in the van. She just hadn't seen the crystal then. They were leaning around it, touching it with their hands and foreheads. Using its power—

—to do what? Kaitlyn thought suddenly. "What are they trying to do?" she shouted to Rob.

"They're trying to destroy our crystal," one of the Fellowship answered. A sturdy woman who was in the outer circle around the fountain. "They've set up a vibration to shatter it. They won't be able to do it, though, not while all our power is protecting it."

"Can we help?" Rob yelled.

The woman just shook her head, looking back at the crystal. But Rob and Kaitlyn both moved past her, struck by a common impulse to get as close as possible to what was happening. They squeezed through the crowd and ended up behind Timon and Mereniang.

Timon's frail body was shaking so hard that Kaitlyn felt a stab of fear. She was shaking herself—not with cold, now, but with the vibrations of the crystal. The ground, the fountain, everything was trembling, as if resonating to a single, terrible note.

"So much—evil. So much—"

It was a gasp, and Kaitlyn could barely hear it. But she saw Timon's lips moving and she caught the words. His lined face was white, his eyes wide and clouded.

"I didn't know," he gasped. "I didn't realize—and to do such things to *children* . . ."

Kaitlyn didn't understand. She looked at Mereniang and saw that the dark woman's face was also twisted with horror. Those blue eyes narrowed and streamed with tears.

Then Kait looked at the gray people.

They were more defined than she'd ever seen them before. It was almost as if they were actually materializing here, as if they might appear physically at any moment. She could see their bodies, their hands—and their faces.

One of them was familiar. Kaitlyn had seen that face before—or at least a picture of it. On a folder labeled SABRINA JESSICA GALLO.

But Mr. Zetes had told her they'd all gone insane. Every one of his first students, everyone in the pilot study.

Maybe he didn't mind them being insane. Maybe it was easier to control them that way. . . .

Kaitlyn could feel tears on her own cheeks. Timon was right. Mr. Zetes was absolutely evil.

And he seemed to be winning. The crystal in the fountain was vibrating ever more frenetically. The kaleidoscope of colors disappearing into the misty gray of the other crystal. She could actually see the corrupted crystal more clearly now.

"Timon, let go!" Mereniang was calling. "You're too old for this! The crystal should be sustaining you, not the other way around."

But Timon didn't seem to hear her. "So evil," he said again and again. "I didn't realize how evil. . . ."

"Rob, we've got to do something!" Kaitlyn shouted.

But it was Timon who answered, in a telepathic voice that cut through the ringing in the web. A voice so strong that Kaitlyn whirled to stare at him.

Yes! We must do something. We must let go of the crystal!

Mereniang was staring, too, her eyes and mouth open. "Timon, if we release it—"

Do it! the telepathic voice roared back. *Everyone, do it now!*

And with that, Timon stepped away, taking his hands off the crystal.

Kaitlyn's head was spinning. She watched as the other members of the Fellowship looked at each other wildly, in obvious distress. Then, suddenly, she saw another figure step back.

It was LeShan, his lynx eyes flashing, holding his empty hands in the air.

Another one of the Fellowship stepped away, and another. Finally only Mereniang was holding on.

Let go! Timon shouted.

The crystal was trembling visibly. The piercing note rang higher and higher in Kaitlyn's ears.

"Let go," Timon whispered, as if his strength had suddenly given out. "Someone—make her . . . She'll be destroyed. . . ."

Rob surged forward. He grabbed Mereniang around the waist and pulled. Her palms came away from the crystal, and they both fell to the ground.

The terrible ringing became a terrible crashing. The sound of a million goblets falling to the floor. A sound that deafened Kaitlyn, echoing in every nerve.

The great crystal was shattering.

It was almost like an explosion, although the only thing flying outward was light. A burst of radiance that left Kaitlyn blind as well as deaf. Imprinted on her eyelids she had a picture of thousands of shards hanging in air.

She fell to her knees, arms wrapped around her head protectively.

When she opened her eyes, the world had changed. The wind was gone. So was the smell.

So were the crystals—both of them. The gray crystal had simply vanished, along with the gray people. The other one, the last perfect crystal in the world, was lying in splinters in the water of the fountain.

Dizzy and unbelieving, Kaitlyn looked around.

Timon was lying on the grass, one hand curled on his chest. His eyes were shut, his face waxen.

Rob was picking himself up from under Mereniang, who was crying.

"Why?" the dark woman demanded. It was what Kait wanted to know herself. "Why, why?"

Timon's eyelids fluttered.

"Take a shard and give it to the children," he whispered.

16

Mereniang looked both bewildered and horrified. She didn't move. But LeShan took two quick steps and thrust a hand into the fountain.

"Here," he said, holding out one of the shards toward Rob.

Rob didn't glance up. He was kneeling by Timon, one hand on the old man's upper chest.

"Hang on," he said. Then he glanced up at Mereniang. "He's so weak! It's as if his life-force has disappeared. . . ."

"The crystal was sustaining him," Mereniang said. Her blue eyes, though still fixed on Timon, were dull. She had withdrawn into herself, arms wrapped around her body. "When it shattered, his life ended."

"He's not dead yet!" Rob said fiercely. He shut his eyes, placing his free hand on Timon's forehead. Kaitlyn could sense the healing energy flowing from him.

"No," Timon whispered. "It's no use, and I need you to listen to me."

"Don't talk," Rob ordered, but Kait went to kneel by the old man. She needed to understand what was happening.

"Why did you do it?" she asked.

Timon's eyes opened. There was a strange serenity in their depths. He even managed something like a smile.

"You were right," he said faintly. "Change is good —or at least necessary. Take the shard."

LeShan was still holding out the crystal. Kaitlyn looked from him to Timon. Then she reached out her hand.

The shard was almost as thick as her wrist and a foot long. It was cold and heavy and the facets were very sharp. One sliced into her thumb when she tested the edge.

"Take it back with you, and do what needs to be done," Timon whispered. His voice was almost inaudible now. Rob was sweating, his hands trembling, but Timon seemed to be fading away.

"Some things are so evil they must be fought. . . ."

A shiver went through Timon's frame, and a strange sound came from his lungs. Death rattle, Kaitlyn thought, too numb to move. It was almost like hearing a soul leave a body.

Timon's eyes were wide, staring at the sky. But now they were unseeing.

Kaitlyn's throat felt tight and swollen. Her eyes filled, tears spilling over. All around her the members of the Fellowship were milling about, like a flock of birds thrown into confusion. They didn't seem to know what to do now that Timon was dead and the crystal shattered.

And Rob's chest was heaving. His hair was dark with sweat, his eyes dark with grief. A healer who had lost the battle.

Kaitlyn scooted over to him, glad to have some problem she could understand. She put her arms around him. She felt a ripple in the newly free web and saw Lewis and Anna come to kneel beside her.

They put their arms around both Kait and Rob. All of them holding on as they had in the blizzard. Clinging to one another because they were all they had.

"All right, you lot!" LeShan was shouting. "Timon's gone, but we're still alive. We're going to have to think for ourselves. And we don't have time to stand around!"

"We're going to have to leave, of course," LeShan said. He seemed to have taken charge while Mereniang was grieving. Kaitlyn was glad; LeShan might be aggressive and quick-tempered, but she found him much easier to understand than the rest of the Fellowship.

They were all standing in the central hallway of the white house. Around them the Fellowship was busying itself, packing and carrying, moving and loading.

"You think Mr. Zetes will attack again," Rob said. It wasn't a question.

"Yes, that was just the beginning. He's removed our defenses—and that was probably all he *could* do at one go. Next time it'll be for the kill."

A tall woman looked in from another hallway.

"LeShan, are the children coming with us? I'm trying to arrange transportation."

LeShan looked at Kait and the others.

"Well?" he said.

No one spoke at first. Then Rob said, "Let me get this clear. Timon's idea was that we should go back down to Mr. Zetes, and use the shard of your crystal to destroy *his* crystal."

"It's the only way to do it," LeShan said. "But that doesn't mean you have to."

"Timon *died* so we could have a shard," Anna said. Her normally gentle face was severe.

"And I *still* don't understand," Kait burst out. "Why did everyone listen to him? You were dead-set against fighting before—what made you all change your minds?"

LeShan's lip curled. "I don't think they all *did* change their minds. They're just used to obeying Timon. He might not have considered himself the leader, but everyone let him do the thinking."

"And he changed his mind because of the attack?" Lewis said uncertainly.

"Because of Sabrina," Kaitlyn said. Everyone looked at her. "Didn't you *see?*" she asked.

Lewis blinked. "Who's Sabrina?"

"Sabrina Jessica Gallo. She was one of the gray people. I didn't realize it before because I couldn't see her face."

"Are you sure?" Rob asked.

"Positive. I saw her clearly this time. And I guess that means the other gray people are the other old students. They all looked young to me."

"That was what Timon sensed," LeShan said. His

lips were still curled slightly, as if he had an unpleasant taste in his mouth. "We all sensed it, everyone who was touching the crystal. The attackers were *children*—none of them over twenty. And their minds were twisted . . . I can't explain it."

"They were insane," Kaitlyn told him rather calmly. "That's what Mr. Zetes said, that the crystal had driven them crazy. And that's why I never thought of him using them to attack us. I had the idea they were in institutions somewhere."

"Maybe Mr. Z got them out," Lewis said hollowly.

LeShan grimaced. "In any case, we could feel their agony—and their evil. None of us realized evil like that still existed in the world. I think *we* had the idea that it died when our country died."

"And you're not going to tell us what that country was, are you?" Kaitlyn asked. She'd been meaning to get the question in since yesterday.

LeShan seemed not to hear her. "If you four go back down to fight this man, it will be dangerous," he said. "I won't pretend otherwise. And you can't rely on any help from us. I've got to make sure all these people get settled somewhere—and by the time I'm free, it may be all over with you."

"Thanks," Rob said dryly.

"If I can help after that, I will. But it's your decision."

"We'd be safe if we went with you?" Kaitlyn asked. She felt almost wistful.

"Reasonably safe. Nobody can promise perfect safety."

Kaitlyn sighed. She looked at Rob, and at Lewis and Anna. They were all looking at one another, too.

Do we really have a choice? Rob asked.

The longer we wait, the stronger Mr. Z will get, Anna said. Her thought smoldered with conviction.

We might as well finish what we started, Lewis put in, sounding resigned. He'd bounced back remarkably quickly from his upset. With his natural resilience and optimism, he was even now hoping for the best in Lydia—Kait could tell.

Kaitlyn had a different reason for wanting to go back. Yes, she wanted to stop Mr. Zetes, but there was something more important.

Gabriel, she told the others.

There was an immediate swell of emotion. Some of it was anger, bewilderment, feelings of betrayal. But there was sympathy, too, and determination—and love.

You're right, Rob thought. *If he really is going to join Mr. Zetes—*

I'm afraid he is, Kaitlyn broke in. *I should have thought of it last night. Meren said that any crystal that produces energy could feed him. And Mr. Z's crystal certainly produces energy.*

You think that's why he left? Anna asked.

I don't know. I doubt that's all of it. But I think he'd rather get energy from a crystal than from people. And the more contact he has with that crystal—

"The worse he'll get," Rob said aloud. "The more like Sabrina and those other poor jerks."

"We've got to stop *that,*" Lewis said, startled.

Rob looked at him, and then smiled. It was just the ghost of his normal grin, but it warmed Kaitlyn immeasurably.

"You're right," he said. "We've got to stop it."

"My parents may be able to help," Anna said. "I'm sure they've been trying."

LeShan said, "I'll arrange your transportation."

That was all he said, but his lynx eyes flashed at Kaitlyn. She had the impression that he was desperately proud of them.

"Wait, there's one more thing, " she said anxiously. "I wanted to ask you before, but I never got the chance. There's this girl back in California. Mr. Zetes put her into a coma somehow—with drugs, we think. I told her brother that we'd ask you for help, but . . ."

Her voice trailed off. She could feel Rob's concern regarding Marisol, and his chagrin over forgetting—but LeShan's face was impassive.

Of course they won't be able to help, she thought. *They're not doctors. I was stupid for even asking . . .*

She didn't want to imagine Marisol's brother's face when she told him.

LeShan was nonchalant. "The perfect crystals had the virtue of curing most diseases," he said. "Even a shard ought to do something to help your friend."

Kaitlyn's breath came out in a rush. She hadn't even realized she was holding it, but suddenly her heart was lighter.

LeShan was walking away, but he glanced back over his shoulder and grinned.

"So it's just us again," Lewis said. They were waiting for LeShan to bring them a guide through the forest. Kaitlyn was carrying her duffel bag, which held her clothes—all dirty by now—and her art kit. She had the crystal shard in her other hand.

"We're the only ones we have to rely on," Kaitlyn agreed.

Anna said, "That's all anybody ever has, really."

"Yeah, but all that driving, all that searching," Lewis said. "All for nothing."

Rob looked at him quickly. "It *wasn't* for nothing. We're stronger now. We know more. And we finally have a weapon."

"Right," Anna said. "We set out to find this place and we did. We wanted to find a way to stop Mr. Z and we have."

"Sure. It's all over but the screaming," Lewis said, but he smiled.

Kaitlyn looked back at the white house, now looted and empty. She was wondering if she *could* have stayed if things had been different. If Gabriel hadn't betrayed them, if the Fellowship were staying, could she have made her home here? Would it have been a place where she could have belonged?

"If we can destroy the crystal, we can cure Gabriel, too," Rob was saying.

Kaitlyn looked at him fondly. No, she thought. I don't belong with the Fellowship. I belong with Rob— and Lewis, and Anna, and Gabriel, too. Wherever they are, I'm home.

"Right," she said to Rob. "So let's go do it. The search is on again."

She looked down at the shard. As a ray of sun broke through the clouds, it flashed like diamond.

ABOUT THE AUTHOR

LISA JANE SMITH is the author of more than twenty books for young adults. She is looking forward to the millennium and wonders what the future will bring. She enjoys computers, mythology, walking in the woods at night, and animals. She lives in northern California, in a rambling house among the trees, and gets some of her best ideas sitting under the stars.

Her Archway trilogies include *The Forbidden Game* and *Dark Visions*.

Don't miss the thrilling conclusion to
DARK VISIONS

VOLUME III: THE PASSION

Gabriel has betrayed his friends and joined the dark psychics. He and Rob seem determined to destroy each other—but Kaitlyn can't let that happen. Pretending to join Mr. Zetes herself, she gambles that love can win Gabriel back from the dark. But she finds herself alone with the enemy— and the final confrontation is coming fast. In the last battle, will Kaitlyn choose Rob or Gabriel— light or darkness?